中国南方著名古典史诗英译丛书

丛书主编　张立玉　起国庆

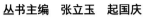

苗族古歌

（汉英对照）

刘德荣　张鸿鑫　项保昌　整理

张立玉　夏　雨　英译

[美] H.W.Lan　审校

出品单位：

中南民族大学南方少数民族文库翻译研究基地

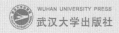

WUHAN UNIVERSITY PRESS

武汉大学出版社

图书在版编目(CIP)数据

苗族古歌 = Ancient Miao Songs：汉英对照/刘德荣,张鸿鑫,项保昌整理;张立玉,夏雨英译.—武汉：武汉大学出版社,2024.3
中国南方著名古典史诗英译丛书/张立玉,起国庆主编
ISBN 978-7-307-24159-6

Ⅰ.苗…　Ⅱ.①刘…　②张…　③项…　④张…　⑤夏…　Ⅲ.苗族—民歌—作品集—中国—古代—汉、英　Ⅳ.I276.291.6

中国国家版本馆 CIP 数据核字(2023)第 228195 号

责任编辑:罗晓华　　　责任校对:汪欣怡　　　版式设计:韩闻锦

出版发行：**武汉大学出版社**　(430072　武昌　珞珈山)
　　　　　(电子邮箱：cbs22@ whu.edu.cn　网址：www.wdp.whu.edu.cn)
印刷：武汉邮科印务有限公司
开本:720×1000　1/16　印张:14.5　字数:175 千字　插页:1
版次:2024 年 3 月第 1 版　2024 年 3 月第 1 次印刷
ISBN 978-7-307-24159-6　　　定价:69.00 元

丛书编委会

序

　　在千古悠悠的历史长河中，中华民族以自己的勤劳和智慧创造了光辉灿烂的古典史诗。古典史诗是一种结构庞大、富有综合性特征的民间长篇叙事诗，一般分为创世史诗、英雄史诗和迁徙史诗三大类，其内容丰富、气势恢弘，在漫长的传承过程中，融进了大量的民间神话、传说、故事、歌谣和谚语等，是一个民族社会生产活动、宗教信仰、风俗习惯和历史文化知识的一种特殊总汇。它经过长期的积累，深深积淀于中华民族的精神文化宝库之中，是千百年来中华民族自尊、自信、自爱、自强意识的重要源泉。它对中华民族文化传统的形成和发展产生了巨大而深远的影响。

　　近年来，为了推动中华文化的国际传播、提升中华文化的影响力、深入挖掘中华文化的精神内核、让中国优秀传统文化走出去，中南民族大学南方少数民族文库翻译研究基地积极对中国南方非遗文化典籍进行对外传播和译介的工作。该基地民族典籍英译捷报频传、硕果累累。先后出版了土家族典籍英译2部，纳西族三大史诗英译3部，"十三五"国家重点图书、国家出版基金项目"中国南方民间文学典籍英译丛书"14部。

　　近日，该翻译研究基地又传来佳音：他们要出版"中国南方著名古典史诗英译丛书"。这套丛书包括十余本，分别是《苗族古歌》《巴塔麻嘎捧尚罗》《厘俸》《阿昌族、德昂族古典史诗》《阿黑西尼摩》《相勐》《阿细的先基》《白族古典史诗（上、下）》《拉祜族创世史诗》《傈僳族叙事诗》《德傣掸登俄》。这些典籍多数入围了国家级非物质文化遗产名录，展示了不同民族的文化。

《苗族古歌》又称"大歌"，作为苗族的创世史诗，它是苗族口传文学的典型代表，也是记录苗族古代社会的一部百科全书。它于2006年5月20日被国务院批准列入第一批国家级非物质文化遗产名录。苗族的各种文化艺术都可以从这里找到它们的源头，《苗族古歌》的内容森罗万象，有苗族的发展史、远古时期的开天辟地、繁衍人类、耕耘劳作、衣食住行、婚丧嫁娶、重建家园，还有苗族人民长期遭受压迫和剥削而反抗以争取自由幸福的生活等内容。它不仅具有历史学、民族学、哲学、人类学的研究价值，还具有教育、审美和娱乐等方面的杰出价值；它是研究远古思想的形象化材料，是苗族历史的艺术写照，也是了解苗族社会习俗的窗口。

《巴塔麻嘎捧尚罗》为傣族创世史诗，是傣族文学的巅峰之作，也是我国南方少数民族创世史诗的经典之作。与《乌沙巴罗》《粘芭西顿》《兰嘎西贺》《粘响》一同被傣族人民称作"五大诗王"。《巴塔麻嘎捧尚罗》融合了傣族本土的神话叙事与外来的佛经叙事，经过历代歌手的不断演述以及文人创编成文、誊抄成本，逐渐实现书面化和系统化，最终形成了15000多行的长篇史诗。这部史诗内容宏大，包括天神英叭诞生、英叭开天辟地、众神诞生、地球毁灭又重生、布桑嘎西与雅桑嘎赛修补天地又捏土造人、葫芦孕育万物、天神制定历法、桑木底教人造屋定居、人类大兴旺、民族迁徙等内容。

《厘俸》是一部在傣族文学史上具有重大意义的英雄史诗，主要叙述了古代英雄海罕和俸改之间的战争，并展示了傣族先民从原始社会解体到奴隶制初期广阔的社会生活。《厘俸》是傣族文学史乃至文化史上一部具有里程碑意义的作品，是傣族形成和崛起期所有重大历史事件、军事行动、社会生活、时代风尚、英雄崇拜、信仰体系以及各种英雄传说的历史积淀和艺术创造的结晶。它具有民族史、民族学、宗教学、文化学、文艺学等多学科的价值，堪称傣族古代社会文化的"百科全书"，是一部不可多得的文化遗产。

《阿昌族、德昂族古典史诗》由阿昌族和德昂族两个民族的史诗组成。阿昌族古典史诗《遮帕麻和遮米麻》是流传于云南省德宏傣族景颇族自治州梁河县的传统民间文学，2006年5月被列入第一批国家级非物质文化遗产名录。《遮帕麻和遮米麻》产生于阿昌族早期，是一部讲述阿昌族先民为了感谢遮帕麻和遮米麻的创世之恩，以及补天缝地、降魔降妖等多次挽救人类的大恩大德的民间文学作品，涵括了创世神话、人类起源神话、洪水神话，也包含了人祖英雄神话。这部长诗同时也形象地反映了人类从母权制向父权制过渡的状况。德昂族古典史诗《达古达楞格莱标》是流传于云南省德宏傣族景颇族自治州的民间文学，2008年被列入第二批国家级非物质文化遗产名录，也是德昂族迄今发掘、整理并出版的唯一一部创世史诗。与其他民族的创世史诗不同，《达古达楞格莱标》情节单纯，始终以万物之源——茶为主线，集中地描写了这一人类和大地上万物的始祖如何化育世界、繁衍人类的神迹，并以奇妙的幻想将茶拟人化，提出人类来源于茶树、德昂族是茶树的子孙的独特观点。

《阿黑西尼摩》是彝族创世史诗，流传于云南省元阳县彝族地区。中文版由施文科、李亮文唱述，罗希吾戈、普学旺翻译，收入《云南少数民族古典史诗全集（上卷）》，并入选"中华大国学经典文库"。全诗由序歌、阿黑西尼摩生万物、人类的起源、天地开始分、叭依定历法、旱灾、洪水泛滥、天地生日、长寿和死亡、婚嫁的起源和演变、祭祀兴起等部分组成,是彝族典籍文化的重要组成部分,具有重要的文化价值和历史价值。该史诗中的"神谱"自成系统,内容丰富,幻想奇特,在阐释天地万物的起源方面独树一帜,对研究彝族原始文化,特别是母体崇拜以及人类母系文化,均具有重要价值。

《相勐》取材于傣族历史上部落战争的重大事件,真实地反映了傣族古代社会由部落林立到部落联盟直至最后形成统一的历史进程,展示了广阔的社会生活,塑造了各种英雄人物,显示了民族崛起期——英雄时代的民族精神。在艺术手法上,作品采用框架叙事结构,即以一个故事贯穿全诗,再以大故事套小故事,使情节的发展变化纷繁又紧扣中心。此外,作品语言清新、优美,充分体现出傣族传统诗歌的独特韵味。《相勐》以其特定的历史价值与艺术成就,被称为傣族最为成熟的一部英雄史诗。

《阿细的先基》是彝族支系阿细人的史诗、彝族四大创世史诗之一,由云南弥勒县西山一带的阿细人民口头流传,以固定的"先基调"演唱而得名。在表现形式上采用"先基调"进行演唱,往往通过对唱提问、对答的方式展开诗篇。句式一般为五言,但到了"求爱"等感情激烈的段落时,间用六言和长短句,以便于抒情。全诗分两部分。第一部分"最古的时候"叙述天地万物的起源和人类早期的生活习俗。第二部分"男女说合成一家"记叙阿细人独特的婚姻和风俗习惯。具有传承意义。

拉祜族创世史诗《牡帕密帕》是拉祜族宗教文化的核心部分之一。拉祜族以"卑咯斯"(Birec)为神,他被认为是宇宙的创造者。《牡帕密帕》记录了对卑咯斯的崇拜方式、神话故事以及人们对神灵的祭祀活动。在拉祜族的历史中，这部史诗被传唱和演绎了几百年，并以其独特的形式和内涵成为了拉祜族宗教文化的重要组成部分，被视为拉祜族文化的瑰宝，它记录了拉祜族的起源、神话传说、社会生活等内容。这一史诗的传承与发展是拉祜族文化的传承与发展的缩影。

其余几本书展示了白族、傈僳族等的风俗习惯、恋爱故事、斗争故事等。《白族古典史诗（上、下）》中的《串权连》《青姑娘》《鸿雁传书》三部长诗是白族文化典籍。《串权连》热情歌颂了一对白族青年的自由恋爱和他们的坚贞爱情，突出表现了白族人民对"指腹为婚"这一残酷的封建婚姻制度的反抗。《青姑娘》则通过反映旧社会一个童养媳的不幸遭遇，揭露和控诉了封建礼教对青年妇女的残酷迫害。《鸿雁传书》描写的是一对青年夫妻，丈夫出门谋生，远离家乡，二人分居两地，他们只有托鸿雁传书，互相倾诉思念之情。《白族古典史诗（上、下）》中的《出门调》主要流传在云南剑川、洱源、兰坪等县和丽江、九河等白族地区，这部叙述诗通篇用第一人称演唱。它集中描写了剑川木匠出门在外的悲苦生活。而《出门恋歌》虽然也描写了男主人公因生活所迫，不得已与心爱的人分离、外出讨生活的情节，但重点是讲述男女主人公从相知相恋到分离后相思成疾，最终欢喜重逢的故事。

《傈僳族叙事诗》中的《生产调》生动形象地反映了傈僳族人民日常的生产劳动，表现了他们勤劳、善良、友爱、互助的民族性格和美好的民族风尚。《盖房调》为傈僳族古老的传统调子，来源于傈僳族盖房子的劳动。它对傈僳族古老的盖房习俗、住房结构、盖房时的劳动场面均做了真实、细致的描绘，这对人们研究傈僳族的社会生活具有重要的参考价值。《种瓜调》流传于怒江傈僳族自治州的碧江、泸水、福贡、贡山等地的傈僳族人民中，是傈僳族口头诗歌中流传比较广、影响较深的作品，诗中所说的南瓜发芽、出苗、串藤、开花、结瓜，实际上指的是男女青年爱情的成长过程。

《德傣掸登俄》是壮族土僚支系中广为流传的一部创世史诗，由开天辟地、洪水淹天、土僚创世、星女下凡四个部分组成。第一部分的内容为：天地是罗扎、罗妞开辟出来的，万物是罗扎、罗妞制造成的；第二部分的内容为：洪水淹天之后，在葫芦里躲过劫难的两兄妹结为夫妻，传下了人种；第三部分的内容为：土僚先民种稻种棉，铸造铁器，创造了美好生活；第四部分的内容为：天上的星女下凡与罗傣结婚，犹如爱神，为此，每年三月初三，土僚都要祭祀星女。整部长诗共两千多行，绝大部分为五言体，叙事奇特、结构紧密、内容丰富、韵味十足，经常由长老在举办红、白喜事时或节日期间吟诵，颇受群众欢迎。现仍广泛流传于红河流域的壮族地区。

这些故事都很引人入胜，都很符合国家文化发展需求，向世人讲述中国故事、传播中华文化，并且讲述的是中国少数民族故事，充分体现了党和国家对各民族的关怀。这些典籍中折射出的文化多样性极大地丰富了世界文化，使世界文化更加丰富多彩、绚丽多姿。因此，民族典籍英译是传播中国文化、文学和文明的重要途径，是中华文化走出去的重要组成部分，是提高文化软实力的重要方式，在文化交流和文明建设中起着不可或缺的作用，对提高中国对外话语权和构建中国对外话语体系、对建设世界文学都有积极意义。

张立玉　起国庆

2023 年 12 月

前 言

　　《苗族古歌》又称"大歌"，作为苗族的创世史诗，它是苗族口传文学的典型代表，也是记录苗族古代社会的一部百科全书。苗族的各种文化艺术都可以从这里找到它们的源头。《苗族古歌》的内容森罗万象，有苗族的发展史、远古时期的开天辟地、繁衍人类、耕耘劳作、衣食住行、婚丧嫁娶、重建家园，还有苗族人民长期遭受压迫和剥削而反抗以争取自由幸福的生活等内容。它不仅具有历史学、民族学、哲学、人类学的研究价值，还具有教育、审美和娱乐等方面的独特价值。它是研究远古思想的形象化材料，是苗族历史的艺术写照，也是了解苗族社会习俗的窗口。《苗族古歌》在苗族社会历史中具有重要的地位，流传于云南文山和红河的苗族居住地，这些诗歌都是苗族人民代代相传的产物，是苗族古文化的光辉结晶。

　　《苗族古歌》记载了苗族灿烂辉煌的远古文化，它于2006年5月20日被国务院批准列入第一批国家级非物质文化遗产名录。远古时期，苗族人民饱受战争之苦，为躲避战乱，进行了多次大迁徙，苗族先民担心各种信息会湮没于历史长河中，便将本民族的历史深藏于清雅、空灵而又雄浑悲怆的古歌当中，留存于民族的记忆里。据文献记载，苗族起源于黄河中下游，其祖先就是与黄帝大战的蚩尤。蚩尤所在的九黎部落在大败之后，逐渐顺着河流，向南、向西迁移，

1

最终形成了现在的苗族。

本次英译版本的中文原文采用的是云南省少数民族古籍整理出版规划办公室编的《云南少数民族古典史诗全集(中卷)》，由云南教育出版社于 2009 年 9 月出版。该版本是由项保昌(苗族)、刘德荣、陶永华(苗族)收集，并由刘德荣、张鸿鑫、项保昌整理而成。

《苗族古歌》是国家级非物质文化遗产，译者在承担该文学作品的翻译工作时，深感责任重大。为此，译者除了查阅大量相关文献之外，还进入文山、红河苗族居住区以及贵州凯里千户苗寨等地进行实地考察，积极地与苗族人民进行沟通和交流，真切地感受和体验苗族文化，并邀请在英汉文化比较领域从事多年研究的威斯康星大学的 H. W. Lan 教授进行全书的审定，以期尽量将译文中的文化误读与误译的程度降到最低，在精益求精的基础上力图使译文忠实于原文，以此来传神达意。《苗族古歌》世代传唱，语言简洁凝练、直抒胸臆，译者采用直译、意译、音译、释译、转换等方法，尽可能将具有苗族特色的语言原汁原味地呈现到英译本中，力图再现原文中的文学效果。

由于译者水平有限，缺乏苗族文化的相关背景，译文的处理难免有不当之处，敬请广大读者批评指正，以便修订时更正。

译者：张立玉　夏雨

2023 年 6 月

目 录

Contents

第一章 宇宙

一、天地

远古的时候，
天是咋个样？
远古的时候，
地是咋个样？

远古的时候，
天是这个样：
混沌一团气，
滚滚翻热浪。

远古的时候，
地是这个样：
模糊一团泥，
摇摆又晃荡。

天上湿漉漉，
像团鸡屎般；

Chapter 1　The Universe

Section 1　Heaven and Earth

A long, long time ago,
What was heaven like?
A long, long time ago,
What was earth like?

A long, long time ago,
Heaven was like this:
A chaotic mass of air,
Heated rolling waves.

A long, long time ago,
Earth was like this:
A blurry ball of mud,
Swaying and shaking.

Heaven was damp,
Like a ball of chicken dung;

地下软绵绵，
像坨鸭粪样。

天有娘来生，
地有爹来养。
四方亲戚啊，
听我摆端详。

天的亲生娘，
姓氏是什么？
地的生身父，
名字叫哪样？

天的亲生娘，
姓氏是菠媛；
地的生身父，
名字叫佑聪。

菠媛来造天，
整整造九天。
她不歇一歇，
造了九重天。

佑聪来造地，
造了十二夜。
他不停一停，
造地十二层。

Earth was soft,
Like a lump of duck manure.

Heaven was born to its mother,
And earth was cared by its father.
People all over,
Listen to me to explain it in detail.

Heaven's birth mother,
What was her name?
Earth's birth father,
What was his name?

Heaven's birth mother
Was called Bo Chi;
Earth's birth father
Was called You Cong.

Bo Chi created heaven
In exactly nine days.
Without resting,
She made the nine levels of heaven.

You Cong created earth
In twelve nights.
Without stopping,
He made the twelve levels of earth.

苗族古歌 Ancient Miao Songs

菠媤和佑聪，
拿天来盖地。
天窄地宽大，
盖地盖不下。

竺妞听说了，
心里很着急：
天盖不下地，
万物没生机。

竺妞管天下，
一副好心肠，
派了两个神，
匆匆来帮忙。

雷鲁和朱幂，
奉了竺妞命，
心里很喜欢，
拿天来盖地。

菠媤和佑聪，
年纪八百岁；
雷鲁和朱幂，
寿满八百年。

四个大神仙，
两女和两男，

Bo Chi and You Cong,
Tried to use heaven to cover earth.
But heaven was narrower than earth,
Could not cover earth.

Zhu Niu heard of this
And became worried.
If heaven did not cover earth,
Nothing had a chance to live.

Zhu Niu managed the world
With a kind heart.
She assigned two gods,
Who hurried to lend a hand.

Lei Lu and Zhu Mi
Took Zhu Niu's order
And, with their happy hearts,
Came to help make heaven cover earth.

Bo Chi and You Cong
Were eight hundred years old;
Lei Lu and Zhu Mi
Were also eight hundred years old.

These four great gods,
Two females and two males,

样子很古怪，
力气大无边。

菠媸和雷鲁，
头发蓬松松，
乌黑又浓密，
像片大森林。

佑聪和朱幂，
腮下长胡须，
胡须拖着地，
可以编草席。

四个大神仙，
驾云又乘风，
两个来南北，
两个来西东。

各方站一个，
好像四座山，
拿天来盖地，
合力又同心。

一个东方拉，
一个西边弹，
一个南方扯，
一个北边按。

Had odd looks
And boundless strength.

Bo Chi and Lei Lu
Had loose hair,
Black and thick,
Like a big forest.

You Cong and Zhu Mi
Had beards from their chins,
Dragging on the ground,
Like the straws for making the strawmats.

These four great gods
Drove clouds and rode winds,
Two going south and north,
Two going west and east.

They each stood at a corner
Like four mountains,
Trying to make heaven cover earth,
And worked together with one heart.

One pulled eastward,
One plucked westward,
One tugged southward,
And one pressed northward.

地有十二层，
拖得起皱纹。
皱纹一条条，
像笼百褶裙。

凹处是湖河，
凸处是山坡。
天地盖严了，
万物能生活。

天是谁来造？
地是谁来造？
他们的姓名，
世代要记牢。

天是菠嫫造，
地是佑聪造。
他们两个神，
心灵手又巧。

拿天来盖地，
哪个来帮忙？
他们的姓名，
世代不能忘。

拿天来盖地，
多亏两个神，

The twelve layers of earth,
Were stretched and wrinkled.
With those wrinkles,
Earth looked like a pleated skirt.

While valleys became lakes and rivers,
Ridges became hills and mountains.
Heaven now completely covered earth,
So myriads of things could live.

Who created the heaven?
Who made the earth?
Their names
Should always be remembered.

Heaven was created by Bo Chi,
And earth was made by You Cong.
These two gods
Were ingenious and deft with their hands.

Making heaven cover earth,
Who lent a hand?
Their names
Should never be forgotten.

Making heaven cover earth,
We should thank the two gods

雷鲁和朱幂，
留下好名声。

过了好多年，
天上通了洞；
过了好多代，
地下裂了缝。

人烟不能生，
草木不能长。
竺妞听说了，
急得心发慌。

谁人来补天？
哪个来补地？
竺妞下决心，
派出亲生女。

两个巧仙女，
来补天和地。
她们怎样补？
说来很稀奇！

两个巧仙女，
手指白生生，
白得像蒜头，
白得像葱根。

Lei Lu and Zhu Mi,
Who were held in high repute by all.

Many years later,
Heaven had holes;
Many generations later,
Earth had cracks.

People could not live,
And vegetations could not grow.
Zhu Niu heard about it
And became flustered.

Who could patch up heaven?
Who could fix up earth?
Zhu Niu made up her mind
To send her own daughters.

Two clever fairies
Came to fix up heaven and earth.
How did they do that?
It was an amazing story!

The two ingenious fairies
Had white fingers,
As white as the garlics,
As white as the scallion roots.

13

拿起金梭子，
穿上银丝线，
东方织三下，
西方织三下。

两个巧仙女，
手指软和和，
软得像麻团，
软得像棉朵。

拿起银梭子。
穿上金丝线，
南方织三下。
北方织三下。

两个巧仙女，
手指细苗苗，
细得像竹枝，
细得像柳条。

拿起铜梭子，
穿上铁丝线，
天边织三下，
地边织三下。

两个巧仙女，
手指细又长，

With gold shuttles in hands,
Using the silver threads,
They wove in the east three times,
Then in the west three times.

The two ingenious fairies
Had soft fingers,
As soft as skeins of linen threads,
As soft as balls of cotton lints.

With silver shuttles in hands,
Using the gold threads,
They wove in the south three times,
Then wove in the north three times.

The two ingenious fairies
Had slender fingers,
As slender as bamboo twigs,
As slender as weeping willow branches.

With copper shuttles in hands,
Using the iron threads,
They wove at heaven's edge three times,
Then wove at earth's edge three times.

The two ingenious fairies
Had slender and long fingers,

长得像芦苇，
长得像香茅。

拿起铁梭子，
穿上铜丝线，
天角织三下，
地角织三下。

金线变黄云，
银线成白云，
铜线化紫云，
铁线作蓝云。

手中五彩线，
织成五彩云。
早晨映天边，
傍晚绕山林。

两个巧仙女，
手巧心又灵，
补好天和地，
世代出了名。

天上没有洞，
地上没有缝。
人烟生起来，
草木也葱茏。

Like the reeds,
Like the lemongrass.

With iron shuttles in hands,
Using the copper threads,
They wove at heaven's corner three times,
Then wove at earth's corner three times.

Gold threads turned into bright clouds,
Silver threads grew into white ones,
Copper threads changed into lilac ones,
Iron threads became blue ones.

Colorful threads in their hands
Were woven into colorful clouds.
They brightened edges of heaven at dawn
And rounded mountain forests at dusk.

The two ingenious fairies,
With deft hands and bright minds,
Patched up heaven and fixed up earth,
Becoming famed forever.

Heaven had no holes,
And earth had no cracks.
Humans began to thrive,
And vegetations also grew verdantly.

二、日月

远古的时候，
天上湿漉漉；
远古的时候，
地下软绵绵。

天像团鸡屎，
地像坨鸭粪。
鸡屎四面流，
鸭粪到处淌。

要使天干燥，
就得造太阳！
要使地干燥，
就得造月亮！

谁来造太阳？
谁来造月亮？
竺妞心里想：
哪个本领强？

还是农董勾，
本领最高强。
派他造太阳，
派他造月亮。

Section 2　The Sun and the Moon

A long, long time ago,
Heaven was damp;
A long, long time ago,
Earth was soft.

Heaven was like a ball of chicken dung,
And earth was like a lump of duck manure.
The chicken dung flowed around,
While the duck manure moved around.

To make heaven dry,
The sun was needed!
To make earth dry,
The moon was necessary!

Who would make the sun?
Who would make the moon?
Zhu Niu thought to herself:
Who was the competent one?

It had to be Nong Donggou,
Who was the most competent.
He should be assigned to make the sun,
And the moon.

太阳怎样造？
什么办法好？
董勾心最灵，
把他难不倒！

他拿起凿子，
东边凿九下；
他拿起锤子，
西边敲九下。

九个石团子，
立刻就凿成。
他把石团子，
抛到半天云。

九个石团子，
变成了太阳。
九个金太阳，
挂在蓝天上。

月亮怎样造？
哪样办法妙？
董勾手最巧，
把他难不倒！

他拿起凿子，
南边凿九下；

How would the sun be made?
What was the best way?
Donggou was the brightest
And was invincible!

He picked up the chisel
And chiseled nine times in the east;
He picked up the hammer
And hammered nine times in the west.

Nine stone balls
Were done at once.
He threw the stone balls
Into the clouds.

Nine stone balls
Became the suns.
The nine golden suns
Were hanging in the blue sky.

How would the moon be made?
What was the best way?
Donggou was the deftest with his hands
And was invincible!

He picked up the chisel
And chiseled nine times in the south;

他拿起锤子，
北边敲九下。

九个石团子，
马上就敲成。
他把石团子，
甩到半天云。

九个石团子，
变成了月亮。
九个银月亮，
挂在蓝天上。

九个金太阳，
像九个姑娘；
九个银月亮，
像九个伙子。

太阳和月亮，
一共十八个。
它们像情人，
成对又成双。

太阳转过去，
月亮追上来，
一个接一个，
追得不歇台。

He picked up the hammer,
And hammered nine times in the north.

Nine stone balls
Were done right away.
He flung the stone balls
Into the clouds.

Nine stone balls
Became the moons.
The nine silver moons
Were hanging in the blue sky.

The nine golden suns
Were like nine girls;
The nine silver moons
Were like nine boys.

The suns and the moons
Were eighteen in all.
They were like lovers,
Staying together in pairs.

When the suns turned around,
The moons followed them around,
One after another,
Chasing without stopping.

太阳跑得快，
月亮追得忙，
形影也不离，
来往在天上。

天不分白日，
地不分黑夜，
上下烫滚滚，
四方热烘烘。

太阳造多了，
月亮造多了，
天像开水煮，
地像烈火烧。

花草烫焦了，
树木烧枯了，
处处冒黄灰，
大地光秃了。

你看农董勾，
心急如火燎，
天南看一看，
天北瞧一瞧。

你看农董勾，
心急如涨潮，

The suns ran fast,
And the moons chased busily,
Inseparable like things and their shadows,
Traversing in heaven.

Heaven had only daylight,
While earth had no night,
Up and down everything burning,
Along with everywhere roasting.

Too many suns had been made,
And too many moons had been made,
Heaven being like boiling waters,
Earth being like burning fires.

With plants scorched,
Trees burned,
Yellow ashes effusing everywhere,
Earth became bald.

Nong Donggou
Looked anxious like the burning fire,
Looking at heaven in the south
Looking at heaven in the north.

Nong Donggou
Looked anxious like the rising tide,

苗族古歌 Ancient Miao Songs

天东望一望，
天西瞄一瞄。

植物枯又黄，
遍地空荡荡。
只有麻秧树，
高耸在山上。

一棵麻秧树，
挺拔又峻峭，
树干硬邦邦，
树枝直苗苗。

好个农董勾，
喜得心花放，
拿定好主意，
两眼闪金光。

你看农董勾，
朝着麻秧树，
迈开两条腿，
匆匆来赶路。

他沿溪涧跳，
他顺山梁跑，

26

Looking at heaven in the east
Looking at heaven in the west.

Plants withered and yellowed,
And earth was bare.
But one Mayang Tree①
Towered high on the mountain.

One Mayang Tree
Was upright and lofty,
Its trunk strong,
Its branches straight.

The great Nong Donggou,
Bursting with joy,
Thought of a good idea,
His two eyes shining with light.

Nong Donggou,
Toward the Mayang Tree,
Started walking
Hurriedly.

He skipped along by the streams,
Ran along the mountain ridges,

---

① A kind of divine tree in ancient Chinese mythology.

浑身淌汗水，
两脚磨起泡。

九十九条沟，
一气跳过了；
八十八个坡，
一下翻过了。

舌燥口更渴，
腰直腿也僵。
呼呼喘着气，
好像拉风箱。

好个农董勾，
不怕累和苦，
挥起大斧头，
砍倒麻秧树。

树干削成弓，
树枝削成箭。
弓箭握在手，
抬头望着天。

农董勾弯弓，
农董勾搭箭，
瞄准金太阳，
射出八支箭。

Till he was drenched in sweat,
Till his feet were blistered.

Ninety-nine ditches
He jumped over all at once;
Eighty-eight hillslopes,
He crossed over without a break.

His mouth was parched,
And his waist and legs were stiff.
Breathing heavily,
He sounded like bellows blowing.

The great Nong Donggou,
Fearless of tiredness and hardships,
Swung a big axe,
And cut down the Mayang Tree.

He trimmed the trunk into a bow,
The branches into arrows.
With the bow and arrows in his hands,
He looked up at the sky.

Nong Donggou drew the bow,
Nocked the arrows,
Aimed at the golden suns,
And shot eight arrows.

箭杆飞上天，
红光亮闪闪，
好像八条龙，
直向云里钻。

一箭中一个，
八箭中八个。
九个金太阳，
只能留一个。

农董勾弯弓，
农董勾搭箭，
瞄准银月亮，
射出八支箭。

箭杆飞上天，
白光亮闪闪，
好像八条蛟，
直往云海蹿。

一箭中一个，
八箭中八个。
九个银月亮，
只能留一个。

一个金太阳，
一个银月亮，

The arrow shafts flew into the sky,

With streaks of shining red light,

Like eight dragons,

Shooting into the clouds.

One arrow hit one sun,

Eight arrows for eight suns.

Nine golden suns,

Only one could stay.

Nong Donggou drew the bow,

Nocked the arrows,

Aimed at the silver moons,

And shot eight arrows.

The arrow shafts flew into the sky,

With streaks of shining white light,

Like eight flood dragons,

Jumping straight into the sea of clouds.

One arrow hit one moon,

eight arrows for eight moons.

Nine silver moons,

Only one could stay.

One golden sun,

One silver moon,

正好配一对，
恰好成一双。

可是箭飞来，
呼呼发响声。
它俩胆子小，
吓得掉了魂。

太阳忙逃跑，
月亮快藏身，
躲到天边去，
不见踪和影。

天黑了七载，
地暗了七年。
上下黑沉沉，
四方阴惨惨。

雀鸟叫喳喳，
不见方向飞；
蜂蝶打转转，
不知进和退。

出门认错路，
回家摸错门。
有水没法汲，
有地不能耕。

Were just right as a pair,
Perfect as a couple.

But the flying arrows
Whooshed around.
They two were so cowardly
That they were terrified out of their wits.

The sun was quick to flee,
And the moon was quick to hide,
Disappeared into the edges of the sky,
Without a trace.

Heaven was dark for seven years,
So was the earth for seven years.
Up and down it was pitch black,
Gloomy within the four directions.

The chirping birds
Could not see where they were flying;
The swirling bees and butterflies
Did not know if they should go forward or back.

While going out, people got lost,
Going home, they went to the wrong door.
There was water that could not be fetched,
And land that could not be farmed.

生活怎么过？
日子怎样奔？
你看农董勾，
气得头发昏。

董勾心发慌，
抱起头在想：
谁去喊太阳？
谁去喊月亮？

想了整七天，
有了好主张：
牛去喊太阳，
牛去喊月亮！

老牛飞上天，
哞哞叫三声。
牛的声音大，
好像雷在滚。

太阳吓得慌，
月亮心又惊，
瑟瑟打着战，
脸色发了青。

太阳躲得稳，
月亮藏得深，

How to stay alive?

How to subsist?

Nong Donggou

Looked overwhelmed with anger.

Donggou was in a panic,

Thinking with his head in his hands:

Who would go to call for the sun?

Who would go to call for the moon?

After thinking for seven days,

He had a good idea:

Let the ox go call for the sun

And call for the moon!

The ox flew to the sky,

Mooed three times.

Its voice was loud,

As if thunders were rolling.

The sun was scared,

And the moon was startled,

Shivering,

And their faces turning blue.

The sun settled itself securely,

And the moon hid itself deeply,

钻进黑云里，
天边去安身。

董勾着了急，
抱起头又想：
谁去喊太阳？
谁去喊月亮？

想了整七夜，
有了好主张：
马去喊太阳，
马去喊月亮！

老马飞上天，
咴咴吼三声。
马的声音大，
仿佛浪翻腾。

太阳吓得慌，
月亮心又惊，
得得发着抖，
浑身冷冰冰。

太阳躲得稳，
月亮藏得深，
钻进黑云里，
天边去安身。

Shot into the black clouds,

And settled at the edges of heaven.

Donggou was worried,

Thinking with his head in his hands again:

Who would go to call for the sun?

Who would go to call for the moon?

After thinking for seven nights,

He had a good idea:

Let the horse go call for the sun

And call for the moon!

The old horse flew to the sky

And neighed three times.

Its voice was loud,

As if waves were rolling.

The sun was scared,

And the moon was startled,

Shivering,

Chills running through their bodies.

The sun settled itself securely,

And the moon hid itself deeply,

Shot into in the black clouds,

And settled at the edges of heaven.

董勾发了愁，
抱起头再想：
谁去喊太阳？
谁去喊月亮？

七天又七夜，
想得脑发胀。
想起老公鸡，
心里亮堂堂：

公鸡声音好，
它去喊太阳。
太阳会出来，
白天有阳光。

公鸡声音好，
它去喊月亮。
月亮会出来，
夜晚有月光。

公鸡喊太阳，
公鸡喊月亮，
公鸡声音好，
比谁都恰当！

公鸡展双翅，
飞飞又跑跑，

Donggou was anxious,

Thinking with his head in his hands again:

Who would go to call for the sun?

Who would go to call for the moon?

After thinking seven days and nights,

His brain became heavy and tight.

Then the idea of the old rooster,

Brightened his heart:

The rooster had a beautiful voice

for calling for the sun.

The sun would reappear,

To shine in the day.

The rooster had a beautiful voice,

For calling for the moon.

The moon would reappear,

To light the night.

The rooster went to call for the sun,

And call for the moon,

Its voice beautiful,

Most appropriate of all!

The rooster spread its wings,

Flying and running,

一日跃千里，
直奔九重霄。

公鸡到天上，
抖抖身上毛。
扬起红脖子，
又把尾巴翘。

喔喔叫三声，
四方都听到。
声音真好听，
好像吹竹箫。

太阳抹抹脸，
月亮伸伸腰，
拨开层层云，
抿嘴眯眯笑。

太阳出来了，
月亮出来了，
一个追一个，
从东往西跑。

白天阳光照，
晚上月亮笑。
天空多明亮，
大地多妖娆。

Leaping forward a thousand miles a day,
Straight to the high sky.

The rooster arrived at heaven,
Shook its feathers,
Stretched its red neck,
And arched its tail.

It crowed three times,
And was heard everywhere.
The voice was so beautiful,
Like a bamboo flute playing.

The sun wiped its face,
And the moon straightened its body,
Pushing aside the clouds,
And stretched their lips in a smile.

The sun came out,
And the moon reappeared,
One after the other,
Running from east to west.

The sun shined during the day,
While the moon smiled at night.
How bright the sky was,
And how enchanting the earth was.

小鸟枝头叫，
蜂蝶花间绕，
寻食又采蜜，
忙碌又热闹。

上山见着路，
过河见着桥，
耕地又汲水，
快乐又逍遥。

没有红公鸡，
太阳不出来；
没有红公鸡，
月亮不出来。

太阳和月亮，
心里很感激：
到底拿什么，
送给红公鸡？

太阳很焦急，
月亮也忧虑：
哪样做礼物，
才能表心意？

太阳和月亮，
想出好主意：
一把金梳子，
正好来送礼！

Chirping birds among the tree branches,
Dancing bees and butterflies amid flowers,
Seeking food and collecting honey,
They hustled and bustled with excitement.

Paths could be seen up the mountains,
And bridges, across the rivers.
Farmlands could be cultivated and irrigated,
Pappiness and ease were everywhere.

Without the red rooster,
The sun would not have reappeared;
Without the red rooster,
The moon would not have returned.

The sun and the moon,
Were very grateful:
What could they use
To show the red rooster their gratitude?

The sun was anxious,
And the moon was worried:
Would there be a gift,
That could show their appreciation?

The sun and the moon,
Thought of a good idea:
A golden comb
would be the best gift!

公鸡接梳子，
心里很满意。
喔喔啼三声，
还了三个礼。

苗家戴梳子，
戴得很整齐。
梳背朝着天，
梳齿挨头皮。

公鸡不会戴，
戴得很奇怪。
梳背挨头皮，
梳齿朝天摆。

一把金梳子，
变成鸡冠子，
远古到现在，
代代传下来。

Accepting the comb,
The rooster was very happy.
Crowing three times,
It repaid their kindness three times.

The Miao women wear combs
Neatly as their decorations
The comb's back face the sky,
Its teeth touching to scalp.

The rooster did not know this,
So it wore it oddly.
The comb's back touched its scalp,
With its teeth facing the sky.

The golden comb
Had become a cockscomb,
From ancient times to now,
From generation to generation.

第二章　人类

一、浑水朝天

天是谁来造？
地是谁来造？
天是菠媭造，
地是佑聪造。

菠媭造的天，
会热也会凉，
会阴也会晴，
会黑也会亮。

佑聪造的地，
有高又有低，
有山又有谷，
有河又有溪。

不知哪一代，
天干整七年。

Chapter 2 Human Beings

Section 1 Floodwater Surging to the Sky

Who created heaven?
Who made earth?
Bo Chi created heaven,
And You Cong made earth.

Bo Chi created heaven,
Which can be hot or cold,
Cloudy or sunny,
Dark or bright.

You Cong made earth,
Which has its high and low points,
Its mountains and valleys,
Its rivers and streams.

Nobody knows during which generation,
A seven-year drought took place.

大树和竹子，
晒成碎面面。

山上光秃秃，
遍地冒黄烟。
泥巴也发烫，
石头起火焰。

竺妞大神仙，
就对盘姑说：
"你快上天去，
求求玛由梭！"

"请她开天门，
放出老黑云，
放出及时雨，
滋润大森林。"

盘姑急起身，
抬脚就攀登。
走得腿发麻，
来到南天门。

见到玛由梭，
话也说不成。

Big trees and bamboos
Were scorched into ashes.

Mountains were bald,
With yellow smokes effusing everywhere.
Mud was scalding,
With stones burning.

The great goddess Zhu Niu
Told god Pan Gu:
"You go to heaven at once
To plead with Ma Yousuo①".

"Entreat her to open the gate of heaven,
To release the black clouds
And a timely rain
To nourish the forest."

Pan Gu set off in a hurry
Climbing on and on.
Her legs were numb
When she came to the Nantian Gate②.

When she met with Ma Yousuo,
She could hardly talk.

---

① The thunder goddess in ancient Miao songs.
② The gate of heaven.

喘了几口气，
才把话说清：

"雷神玛由梭，
你有菩萨心。
天干地冒火，
请你来照应！"

"赶快开天门，
放出老黑云，
放出及时雨，
滋润大森林！"

雷神玛由梭，
点头来答应。
张嘴吼三声，
雷声轰隆隆。

雷神玛由梭，
一点不怠慢。
眼睛眨一眨，
天空闪一闪。

有了雷和电，
乌云滚成团，

Having caught her breath,
She finally said clearly:

"Thunder goddess Ma Yousuo,
You have the heart of a Bodhisattva.
With our dry sky and burning earth
Would you please help?"

"Please open the gate quickly
To release the black clouds
And a timely rain
To nourish the forest!"

Thunder goddess Ma Yousuo
Nodded to accept the request.
She roared three times,
And the thunder rumbled.

Thunder goddess Ma Yousuo
Acted without delay.
As soon as she blinked her eyes,
Lightning flashed across the sky.

Following thunder and lightning,
The black clouds rolled into cloud balls,

一阵狂风吹，
遍地落雨点。

狂风有多大？
山梁被吹垮，
山坡被吹斜，
山谷吹成洼。

雨点有多大？
有的像陀螺，
有的像坛子，
有的像囤包。

雷神玛由梭，
她说天太旱，
下雨就下够，
下个不断线。

大雨下多久？
下了三个春，
又下三个冬，
下了整三年。

好心办坏事，
大地遭水淹。
树木沉水底，
山梁看不见。

A gale gusted through,
And the rain started everywhere.

How strong was the gale?
Mountain ridges collapsed,
Hillsides tilted,
And valleys dented.

How big were the raindrops?
They were like tops,
Like vats,
And like grain warehouses.

Thunder goddess Ma Yousuo said,
It was too dry
And, for the rain to be enough,
It must rain nonstop.

How long did the rain last?
It lasted three springs,
Three winters,
Three whole years.

The good intention ended in bad things,
Ended in the earth being flooded.
Trees sank to the bottom of the water,
And mountains vanished from the sight.

天连着了水，
水接着了天。
四周白茫茫，
波浪翻滚滚。

天上浑三年，
地下浊三年，
天上和地下，
浑浊难分辨。

草不剩一棵，
叶不留一片，
万物齐淹死，
遍地是灾难。

只有两兄妹，
福哥和福妹，
跳进大葫芦，
灾难才避免。

福哥和福妹，
相依又相伴，
死里来逃生，
漂到天际边。

葫芦浮水面，
晃荡撞着天，

The sky was connected to the water,
While the water reached up to the sky.
The world was shrouded in endless whiteness,
And the waves were rolling.

The sky was cloudy for three years,
And the earth was turbid for three years,
The sky and the earth were
Hard to tell apart.

Not a blade of grass was left,
And not a leaf was spared.
Everything was drowned,
Everywhere a disaster.

Only two siblings,
Brother Fu and Sister Fu
Jumped into a big gourd
And survived the catastrophe.

Brother Fu and Sister Fu
Relied on each other,
Escaped death,
As they drifted to the edge of the sky.

When the gourd surfaced,
It shook so hard that it hit the sky,

轰隆一声响，
震得天打战。

竺妞的牛圈，
竺妞的猪圈，
震得嘎嘎响，
墙歪柱子偏。

竺妞惊醒了，
睁眼四下看，
没有看清楚，
心中很不安。

竺妞转过头，
急得大声喊：
"管家理财的，
快听我语言！

"赶紧开天门，
出去看一看，
看看是哪样，
撞着这边天。

"赶紧开天门，
出去看一看，
哪样震着了，
牛圈和猪圈。"

And with a bang
The sky was shaken, too.

Zhu Niu's cattle pen,
And Zhu Niu's pigsty,
Squeaked with the shake,
The walls and columns were damaged.

Startled awake,
Zhu Niu opened her eyes and looked around,
But she could not see clearly,
And became very uneasy.

Zhu Niu turned her head,
And Shouted loudly in a hurry:
"Steward! Steward!
Listen!"

"Hurry and open the gate of heaven,
To see
What or who
Hit the sky?"

"Hurry to open the gate of heaven,
To see
What damaged
The cattle pen or the pigsty?"

管家理财的，
开了天门看，
满眼是汪洋，
洪水顶着天。

管家理财的，
惊得傻了眼，
慌忙向竺妞，
仔细说一遍：

"禀告竺妞仙，
天下遭水淹，
满眼是汪洋，
洪水顶着天！"

竺妞下命令：
"铁柱取四根，
东南和西北，
各方钉一根！"

竺妞又吩咐：
"铜柱取四根，
东西和南北，
各方钉一根！"

把天四只角，
钉出八个洞。

The steward
Opened the gate of heaven,
And saw a world of waters,
The flood reaching up to the sky.

The steward
Was stunned,
And hurried back to report to Zhu Niu
Everything that he had seen:

"My lord,
The earth has been flooded,
There is water wherever the eye can see,
The floodwater is pushing against the sky!"

Zhu Niu gave an order:
"Take four iron pillars,
East and south, as well as west and north,
And drill one through in each direction!"

Zhu Niu gave another order:
"Take four copper pillars,
East and west, as well as south and north,
And drill one through in each direction!"

At four corners of heaven,
Eight holes were drilled.

洪水慢慢落，
一天落一寸。

管家理财的，
又忙来报告：
"禀告竺妞仙，
洞洞太少了。"

"八个落水洞，
洪水落不赢。
快快想办法，
再打落水洞！"

竺妞忙吩咐：
"银刀九十把，
戳在坡头上，
戳在山洼洼！"

竺妞又吩咐：
"金刀九十把，
戳在石缝里，
戳在岩壁下！"

银刀和金刀，
遍地都戳满。
高山和平地，
处处是落洞。

The floodwater receded slowly,
An inch a day.

The steward
Came hurriedly to report again:
"My lord,
The holes are too few."

"There are eight draining holes,
But the floodwater is receding too slowly.
Something else is needed quickly
To drill more holes!"

Zhu Niu commanded again right away:
"Take ninety silver swords,
Stick them into the mountaintops
And into the valley floors!"

Zhu Niu commanded again:
"Take ninety gold swords,
Stick them into the cracks of the rocks
And into the bottom of the cliffs!"

With silver and gold swords
Stuck into the ground everywhere.
High mountains and flat lands
Were full of draining holes.

处处是落洞，
洪水全消尽。
现出高山顶，
现出大森林。

葫芦落下来，
咔嗒一声响，
搁在昆南山，
震得山摇晃。

福哥和福妹，
闷在葫芦里，
葫芦盖得严，
四周黑漆漆。

鸡儿啄蛋壳，
才能钻出来；
福哥割葫芦，
才能钻出来。

福哥拿把刀，
使劲割葫芦。
前头割个洞，
后头割条缝。

兄妹两头钻，
一个脸朝西，
一个脸朝东，
相对笑嘻嘻。

Everywhere was full of draining holes
That drained the floodwater completely.
Mountaintops reemerged,
And big forest reappeared.

The gourd lowered down,
With the sound of a click,
Landed on the Kunnan Mountain
And gave the mountain a shake.

Brother Fu and Sister Fu
Were quiet in the gourd
That was sealed tightly,
And was completely dark inside.

Chicks must peck their way
Out of the eggshell;
Brother Fu must carve their way
Out of the gourd.

He took a knife,
Carved hard on the gourd.
He carved a hole in the front
And a crack in the back.

The brother and sister escaped from each end,
One facing the west,
One facing the east,
And they smiled when seeing each other.

二、兄妹造人烟

天下遭灾难，
竺妞心发慌，
吃也吃不饱，
睡也睡不香。

竺妞下命令：
"再去察灾情，
看看天底下，
有人没有人。"

管家理财的，
赶紧开天门。
看看天底下，
不见哪样人！

小虫灭了迹，
雀鸟绝了种。
只有昆南山，
还有两个人。

一个是福哥，
一个是福妹，
兄妹两个人，
真是孤零零！

Section 2　Siblings Making Humans

The world suffered a disaster,
Which got Zhu Niu worried,
Who was unable to eat well
Or sleep soundly.

Zhu Niu gave another order:
"Inspect the situation again
To see whether under the sky
There is anyone."

The steward
Opened the gate quickly,
Looked down,
But saw very little!

Insects had disappeared,
And birds had died out.
Only on the Kunnan Mountain
Two people were left.

One was Brother Fu,
While the other was Sister Fu,
Brother and sister
Live lonely together!

苗族古歌 Ancient Miao Songs

福哥和福妹，
相伴又相依，
岩洞是房子，
野菜来充饥。

福哥和福妹，
一刻也不离，
生活七百年，
越过越亲密。

天上静悄悄，
地下冷清清。
人间没烟火，
树梢没鸟啼。

竺妞叫福哥，
竺妞喊福妹：
"人烟断绝了，
你俩成夫妻！"

竺妞说千回，
福哥不吭声；
竺妞说万遍，
福妹不答应。

竺妞苦相劝，
说得多殷勤。

Brother Fu and Sister Fu
Depended on each other,
Living in the cave,
Living on wild vegetations.

Brother Fu and Sister Fu
Never went away from each other,
They lived seven hundred years,
Growing closer and closer to each other.

The sky was quiet,
And the earth was dreary.
The world had no trace of life,
And the treetops had no bird singing.

Zhu Niu told the Brother Fu,
And Sister Fu,
"Human beings will die out
Unless you become husband and wife!"

Zhu Niu said a thousand times,
But Brother Fu did not respond;
Zhu Niu said ten thousand times,
But Sister Fu would not agree.

Zhu Niu tried hard to persuade them,
But no matter how sincere she sounded,

福哥和福妹，
一点不动心！

福妹最机智，
福妹最聪明。
一番知心话，
说给福哥听：

"福哥呀福哥，
主意要拿定。
你我亲兄妹，
咋个能成亲?"

"你去四面瞧，
你去八方看，
天有这样大，
地有这样宽。"

"可能还有人，
没有遭水淹，
逃进山旮旯，
躲过大灾难。"

"找出他们来，
地上有人烟。
传宗又接代，
洪荒变人间。"

Brother Fu and Sister Fu,
Were unpersuaded!

Sister Fu was the most quick-thinking
And was the most quick-witted.
She had a heart-to-heart
With her brother:

"My dear brother,
We must stick to our decision.
As blood siblings,
How can we marry each other!"

"Go look around
In all directions,
Under the sky so vast,
On the earth so wide."

"There may be some,
Who survived the flood,
Hiding in some nook and cranny,
Spared by the disaster."

"Find them out,
So that there is life on the earth.
Humans can procreate,
And restore life to the flood-destroyed land."

"竺妞不来说，
竺妞不来缠。
你我两兄妹，
心中也安然。"

哥听妹的话，
走北又串南，
往东又奔西，
整整走七年。

天空没鸟飞，
洞里没虫眠，
地上不见人，
四处没火烟。

竺妞又来说：
"要听我相劝，
你俩不成亲，
天下绝人烟！"

兄妹一起答：
"这事很难办，
兄妹成夫妻，
笑话传千年！"

竺妞耐心说：
"洪水来泛滥，

"Zhu Niu will not be here to nag us,
And will not be here to bother us.
You and me, brother and sister,
Can then enjoy our peace of mind."

Brother Fu listened to his sister,
Went to the north and the south
To the east and the west
For seven full years.

With no bird flying in the sky,
No insect sleeping in the caves,
No human appearing on the earth,
There was no sight of life anywhere.

Zhu Niu said again,
"Take my advice,
If you two will not get married,
The human race will be extinct!"

The brother and sister answered together:
"This is a difficult matter,
Siblings becoming husband and wife
Will be the butt of the joke forever!"

Zhu Niu said patiently:
"Because of the flood,

世界成汪洋，
万物遭劫难。"

"你俩不成亲，
人种把根断；
人种断了根，
大地成荒原。"

"我有好办法，
你俩试试看：
同栽鸳鸯树，
我自有公断。"

"妹在河这边，
哥在河那边，
一人栽一棵，
看看可相连。"

"倘若树相连，
就是好姻缘。
你俩就成亲，
不得再翻脸！"

"如果不相连，
不是好姻缘。

the world has turned into an ocean,

And everything was devastated."

"If you do not marry each other,

Humans will die out;

If humans become extinct,

The earth will become a wasteland."

"I have a good idea

That you two can try:

Plant Yuanyang① trees at the same time,

And let me interpret the sign."

"The sister will plant on this side,

And the brother, the other side of the river.

Each will plant one tree

To see if the two trees will connect."

"If they do,

It is a sign that your marriage is meant to be.

You then should marry each other

With no more delay!"

"If the trees do not connect,

It is a sign that marriage is not meant to be.

---

① The Chinese pronunciation of lovebirds.

你俩不成亲，
我也就心甘！"

听了这番话，
哥妹难决断。
如果栽了树，
又怕树相连。

如果不栽树，
竺妞又来缠。
管它连不连，
还是试试看。

妹在河这边，
哥在河那边，
两人来栽树，
栽下七百天。

两棵鸳鸯树，
长在河两边。
中间隔条河，
河有百丈宽。

阳光映树叶，
暖风抚树干，
河水润树根，

You two do not marry,
And I lose fair and square!"

On hearing this,
The brother and sister faced a dilemma.
If they planted the trees,
They feared the trees would connect.

If they did not plant the trees,
They worried that Zhu Niu would return.
They decided to take their chances
And give it a try.

The sister was on one side of the river,
While the brother, on the other side,
The two planting the trees
That grew for seven hundred days.

The two Yuanyang trees
grew on the two sides of the river.
In between was a river,
More than a hundred zhang① wide.

The sun shined on the leaves,
The warm wind caressing the trunks,
The riverwater moistening the roots,

---

① A unit of length equal to 3.3333 meters.

苗族古歌 Ancient Miao Songs

云彩抹树尖。

两树同齐长，
高耸入云端。
挺拔又秀丽，
迎风舞翩翩。

树枝千百条，
伸到河中间，
活像千双手，
紧紧抱一团。

两棵鸳鸯树，
并成一棵树，
树叶紧相挨，
树枝紧相连。

竺妞咧嘴笑，
接着开了言：
"两树紧相连，
这是好姻缘。"

"你们兄妹俩，
要听我相劝。
赶快来成亲，
不要再拖延！"

76

and the clouds touching the treetops.

The two trees had the same heights,

Towering into the clouds.

They were tall and beautiful,

Dancing and swaying in the wind.

Hundreds and thousands of branches

Reached to the middle of the river,

Like a thousand hands

Holding tightly to each other.

The two Yuanyang trees

Merged into one,

With the leaves next to each other

And the branches linked to each other.

Zhu Niu smiled,

And she then said:

"The two trees are closely connected,

A sign the marriage is meant to be."

"You two siblings,

Please take my advice.

Hurry to get married

With no more delay!"

福哥闭着嘴，
福妹不开言，
还是不动心，
成亲事难办！

竺妞一眨眼，
又生计一端：
"一次怕是假，
再试二次看。"

"二次试哪样？
来滚银项圈，
再丢花围腰，
看看可灵验。"

"妹拿花围腰，
哥拿银项圈，
同往山下丢，
看它可相连。"

"如果两相连，
就是好姻缘。
你们就成亲，
一起造人烟。"

"如果不相连，
不是好姻缘。

Brother Fu was silent,

And Sister Fu did not speak,

Still not wanting to do it,

Making the marriage hard!

Zhu Niu, with a spark in her eye,

Thought of another idea:

"The sign of one test may be false,

So let's try again."

"How to try a second time?

Rolling the silver neckring,

Then throwing the colorful apron,

May also produce signs."

"The sister will take the colorful apron,

And the brother, the silver neckring,

To throw down the mountainside together

To see if they will connect."

"If they do,

It is a sign that the marriage is meant to be.

Then you get married,

To procreate together for the human race."

"If they do not connect,

It is a sign the marriage is not meant to be.

你们不成亲，
我也不纠缠！"

听了这番话，
兄妹齐祝愿：
"围腰和项圈，
不要再相连。"

"项圈滚下河，
围腰飘上天，
相隔千万里，
上下各一边！"

妹拿花围腰，
哥拿银项圈。
妹妹上东山，
哥哥上西山。

妹丢花围腰，
哥滚银项圈。
围腰飘飘落，
项圈轱辘转。

到了山脚下，
围腰和项圈，
结合在一起，
相挨又相连。

You do not marry each other,
And I will not bother you anymore!"

On hearing this,
The brother and sister both made a wish:
"Apron and neckring,
Please do not connect."

"Hope the neckring roll down the river,
And the apron fly into the sky,
Separated by thousands of miles,
Going your own ways up or down!"

While the sister took the colorful apron,
The brother took the silver neckring.
The sister went to the east mountain,
And the brother, to the west mountain.

The sister threw the colorful apron,
And the brother rolled the silver neckring.
The apron descended,
And the silver neckring rolled down.

At the foot of the mountain,
The apron and the neckring
Came together as one,
Adjacent and connected to each other.

两根红飘带，
相交又相缠，
扭成两个结，
绞住银项圈。

竺妞哈哈笑：
"二次也灵验，
不要推辞了，
快把亲事办！"

任你说千回，
任你道万遍。
福哥和福妹，
主意终不变：

"谢谢竺妞仙，
莫再来相劝，
我们亲兄妹，
成亲难上难！"

竺妞皱皱眉，
又长巧心眼：
"二次怕是假，
再试三次看。"

"三次试哪样？
来丢针和线。

The two red ribbons,

Intersected and intertwined,

Twisted into two knots,

Tied to the silver neckring.

Zhu Niu smiled and said:

"The second test has shown the same sign,

So don't refuse,

And hurry to get the marriage done!"

It mattered not if she said it thousands

Or tens of thousands of times.

Brother Fu and Sister Fu,

Would not change their minds:

"Thank you, goddess Zhu Niu,

But do not try to persuade us again,

For we blood siblings

Could hardly get married!"

Zhu Niu frowned

And then had another idea:

"Since two tests may still be false,

Let's attempt a third time."

"What to try for the third time?

Throw the needle and thread.

妹妹拿金针，
哥哥拿银线。"

"同向河里丢，
看针可穿线。
如果针穿线，
就是好姻缘。"

"你俩就成亲，
共同造人烟。
金针不穿线，
不是好姻缘。"

"你俩就分开，
我也不来劝。
到底可是真，
赶紧来试验！"

听了这番话，
兄妹齐哀叹：
"这个竺妞仙，
真是太讨厌！"

"几番瞎操心，
到底为哪般？
再试这一回，
再过这一关！"

The sister will take the gold needle,
While the brother, the silver thread."

"You both throw them into the river
To see if the needle will be threaded.
If the needle is threaded,
It is a sign that the marriage is meant to be."

"Then you two should marry,
To procreate for the human race together.
If the gold needle is not threaded,
The marriage is not meant to be."

"Then, you two may seperate from each other,
I won't stop you.
What is meant to be?
Try and find it out!"

On hearing this,
The brother and sister sighed together:
"This goddess Zhu Niu,
What a nuisance!"

"Worried and worried,
What is she doing?
We will try this one more time,
And to go through one more test!"

"老天来保佑，
菩萨来照看。
但愿那金针，
不要穿银线！"

福妹拿金针，
福哥拿银线。
福妹在南边，
福哥在北边。

中间隔条河，
河水流潺潺。
哥妹向河里，
丢下针和线。

金针和银线，
落在河中间。
针在前边漂，
线在后边赶。

满河金晃晃，
水花亮闪闪。
金针打旋涡，
银线打转转。

金针漂得远，
看也看不见，

"Hope the heaven,
And Bodhisattva bless us.
Make that silver thread
Not thread the gold needle!"

Sister Fu took the gold needle,
While Brother Fu took the silver thread.
Sister Fu was in the south,
While Brother Fu was in the north.

In between was a river,
Gurgling with its water.
The brother and the sister,
Threw the needle and thread into the river.

The gold needle and silver thread
Fell into the middle of the river.
The needle floated ahead,
With the thread chasing behind.

The river glittered with the golden light,
And the water was sparkling.
The gold needle swirled,
And the silver thread whirled.

The gold needle drifted far away,
Out of sight,

钻进浪花里，
躲过银丝线。

银线追上来，
抬头四处看，
为了找金针，
不怕巨浪翻。

金针晃一晃，
银线就看见，
忽地蹿上去，
跟在针后边。

银线喘口气，
一下飞上前，
像条小银龙，
钻进针眼眼。

银线穿了针，
金针连了线。
多少鱼和虾，
一起跑来看。

竺妞笑哈哈：
"银线穿金针，
金针连银线，
就是好姻缘！"

Under the waves,
Dodging the silver thread.

The silver thread kept up,
Raising its head to look around,
In search of the gold needle,
Fearless of the billows.

The flickers of the gold needle
Caught the eye of the silver thread,
Which then leapt forcefully,
To keep up with the gold needle.

The silver thread caught its breath,
Flew forward,
Like a small silver dragon,
And threaded the needle.

The silver thread threaded the needle,
Which was now connected to the thread.
Many, many fishes and shrimps,
Came to take a look.

Zhu Niu smiled and said:
"Silver thread threading the gold needle,
Gold needle tied to the silver thread,
It is a sign that the marriage is meant to be!"

"你们兄妹俩，
快把亲事办。
三回为定准，
莫再把理搬！"

福哥和福妹，
羞得红了脸。
二人暗商量，
轻声来叙谈：

"我们兄妹俩，
看来是姻缘。
天家来撮合，
只好照着办。"

妹说照着办，
哥说照着办。
兄妹要成亲，
惊动众神仙。

天母和地公，
菠媸和佑聪；
天神和地神，
雷鲁和朱幂。

四个大神灵，
四方来汇拢，

"You brother and sister,
Hurry up to get married.
Three times are a definite sign,
No more wrangling!"

Brother Fu and Sister Fu
Blushed with bashfulness.
They talked to each other
And then spoke softly:

"We brother and sister
Seem to be meant to get married.
Since this is the will of heaven,
We have to act accordingly."

The sister agreed,
So did the brother.
The news that the brother and sister were getting
married,
Excited the immortals.

Mother of heaven and Lord of earth
Were Bo Chi and You Cong;
The god of heaven and the god of earth,
Were Lei Lu and Zhu Mi.

These four great gods
Came from the four directions,

为了哥和妹，
共同来主婚。

菠媭送金帐，
佑聪送银床，
雷鲁送铜镜，
朱幂送玉盆。

星星当明珠，
云彩作褶裙，
长虹当项圈，
山雾作围巾。

海水酿仙酒，
百果制糕饼。
百兽来做客，
百鸟来陪宾。

请来九大仙，
吹起金芦笙；
请来九仙女，
对歌又弹琴。

竺妞在中间，
自称是媒人。

To preside over the wedding of
The brother and the sister.

Bo Chi gifted them with a gold bed-net,
You Cong, a silver bed,
Lei Lu, a bronze mirror,
And Zhu Mi, a jade basin.

Stars were used as their bright pearls,
Clouds, their pleated skirts,
Rainbows, their neckring,
Mountain mists, their scarfs.

Seawater was used to brew the fairy wine,
And hundreds of berries, to make cakes.
Hundreds of beasts came as guests,
And hundreds of birds came as accompanying guests.

Nine immortals were invited
To play the Jinluda①;
Nine fairies were invited
To sing and play the Yueqin②.

The self-claimed matchmaker
Zhu Niu was in the middle.

---

① A Miao instrument similar to a reed-pipe wind instrument.
② A stringed musical instrument commonly loved by Miao.

出面主婚事，
忙也忙不赢。

哥妹拜天地，
双双成了亲。
一起入洞房，
众神笑盈盈。

结婚七年整，
福妹怀了孕，
怀了七个冬，
又怀七个春。

胎儿生下地，
形状不像人，
像个大南瓜，
浑身圆滚滚。

没头又没脑，
没手又没脚，
分明是坨肉，
看起真吓人！

福妹问福哥：
"福哥呀福哥，
生个怪娃娃，
你看咋个整？"

She hosted the wedding,
Too busy to stop.

After thanking heaven and earth,
The brother and sister were married.
They went to the bridal chamber together,
All the gods smiling.

Exactly seven years after their marriage,
Sister Fu was pregnant,
Which went for seven winters
And seven springs.

The baby was born
But it was not like a person in shape,
Was rather like a big pumpkin,
Round all over.

It had no head and brain,
Or hands and feet,
A lump of flesh,
Looking scary!

Sister Fu asked Brother Fu:
"My dear brother,
With this strange baby,
What should we do?"

福哥出了门，
去问两个神，
菠箐和佑箐，
他们能说清。

菠箐和佑箐，
两个万事通。
能解天下谜，
能卜吉和凶。

"菠箐呀菠箐，
佑箐呀佑箐，
福妹生怪胎，
哪里是个人!"

"像个大南瓜，
浑身圆滚滚。
我来问你们，
到底咋个整?"

菠箐和佑箐，
一起嘱咐道：
"快把那怪胎，
砍成肉片片。"

"砍成多少片?
整整一百片，

Brother Fu went out
To ask the two gods,
Bo Shao and You Shao,
To find out.

Bo Shao and You Shao,
Both were omniscient.
They could solve all worldly mysteries
And divine the future."

"Great Bo Shao,
And great You Shao,
Sister Fu gave birth to a freak,
Not a person!"

"Like a big pumpkin,
Its whole body is round.
I come to consult you,
What should be done?"

Bo Shao and You Shao
Said together:
"Hurry up and cut that freak
into slices of flesh."

"How many slices?
Make it one hundred,

不准多一片，
不准少一片。"

"东边丢一片，
西边丢一片，
南边丢一片，
北边丢一片……"

福哥提起刀，
心烦意又乱。
只顾嚓嚓砍，
懒得数片片。

福妹着急了，
生怕砍多了，
又怕砍少了，
急忙来阻拦：

"福哥呀福哥，
数数再来砍，
照准数目砍，
免得生麻烦！"

福哥停住刀，
来数肉片片。
正好九十九，
还剩一大片。

Not a slice more,
Or a slice less."

"Throw one slice to the east,
One to the west,
One to the south,
One to the north..."

Brother Fu picked up a knife,
Upset and confused.
He just sliced away,
Too grieved to count the pieces.

Sister Fu became worried,
Fearful of making too many pieces,
Or too few,
And hurried to stop him:

"My dear Brother Fu,
Count and then continue,
Aiming at the number,
To avoid trouble!"

Brother Fu stopped slicing
And counted the slices.
The number was exactly ninety-nine,
With a large piece left.

总数合起来，
足足一百片，
没有多一片，
也不少一片。

福哥和福妹，
拿起肉片片，
东西和南北，
各处丢一片……

过了一晚上，
四处是人烟。
户户有笑声，
家家冒炊烟。

一家两个人，
一女配一男，
成双又成对，
日子香又甜。

在园子边的，
他家就姓王；
在柳树边的，
他家就姓杨。

在桃林边的，
他家就姓陶；
在河水边的，
他家就姓何。

The total added up
To exactly one hundred slices,
With not one more,
Or one less.

Brother Fu and Sister Fu
Picked up the slices of flesh,
East and, west, as well as south and north,
They scattered the pieces everywhere...

After one night,
People appeared everywhere.
Every household was filled with laughter,
Every chimney emitting cooking smoke.

Each family had two people,
A female and a male.
They lived as a couple,
And their lives were happy and sweet.

Next to the garden
Lived the Wang family;
Next to the willow tree
Lived the Yang family.

Next to the peach tree grove
Lived the Tao family;
Next to the river,
Lived the He family.

近李子树的，
他家就姓李；
在石头旁的，
他家就姓石……

大的那片肉，
变成了汉族。
汉族人最多，
分布在各处。

小的肉片片，
变些哪样族？
壮苗瑶彝傣，
还有仡佬族……

地上有人了，
总共一百家。
各家一个姓，
成了百家姓。

人烟众多了，
生产又劳动。
来往要交换，
买卖做生意。

杨雅和农雅，
开街又设城。

Living next to the li① trees,
The family took the surname Li.
Living next to the shi②,
The family took the surname Shi...

That large piece of flesh
Became the Han ethnic group.
The Han ethnic group with the largest population
Distributed everywhere.

The small slices of flesh,
What ethnic groups have they become?
Zhuang, Miao, Yao, Yi, Dai,
And the Gelao ethnic group.

The earth now had people,
Altogether a hundred families.
Each family had a surname,
A total of a hundred surnames.

There were many people,
Producing and working together.
Living with each other required trade,
So business was born.

Yang Ya and Nong Ya
Created streets and set up cities.

---

① The Chinese pronunciation of plum.
② The Chinese pronunciation of stone.

贸易有集市，
赶场有定期。

六天赶一次，
老少都到齐。
卖了豆麻油，
又买猪鸭鸡。

杨雅和农雅，
两个又规定：
三百六十天，
满了是一年。

一年有起始，
新春是开头，
家家过春节，
吃肉又喝酒。

婚姻嫁娶时，
对歌吹竹笛。
三亲和六戚，
共同来贺喜。

There were fairs for trade
And the fairs had regular schedule.

A fair was held every six days,
People of all ages being present.
Sesame oil was sold,
And bought were pigs, ducks, chickens.

Yang Ya and Nong Ya
Stipulated also:
Three hundred and sixty days
Made a full year.

A year had a beginning,
Which was the Spring Festival.
Every family celebrated it
By eating meat and drinking wine.

At the time of marriage,
Duets were sung and the bamboo flutes were played,
All relatives
Came together to celebrate.

第三章　农事

一、造田造地

远古的时候，
没有田和地。
哪个来造田？
哪个来造地？

远古的时候，
没有田和地。
竺妞来造田，
竺妞来造地。

田造在哪里？
地造在哪里？
哪里土最肥，
才好造田地。

竺妞坐着想，
想也想不起；

Chapter 3   Agriculture

Section 1   Farmland Making

A long, long time ago,
There was no farmland or field.
Who would make the farmland?
Who would make the field?

A long, long time ago,
There was no farmland or field.
Zhu Niu came to make the farmland
And the field.

Where should the farmland be made?
Where should the field be made?
The most fertile soil
Was for farmland making.

Zhu Niu sat and thought,
But she had no idea.

竺妞睡着想，
想也想不起。

竺妞想三天，
想得心焦急；
竺妞想七夜，
想得着了迷。

脑门打了皱，
头顶脱了皮，
嘴皮开了裂，
脚瘦手杆细。

老是在家想，
想得百病起。
要找好地方，
还得花力气。

竺妞爬起来，
走到深山里。
从南找到北，
从东找到西。

一只小松鼠，
嘴里含板栗。
竺妞追松鼠，
追了七百里。

Zhu Niu lay down and thought,
but she still had no idea.

Zhu Niu thought for three days,
Three days of anxiety;
Zhu Niu thought for seven nights,
Seven days of fascination.

As her forehead developed wrinkled,
The top of her head peeled off,
Her lips became chapped,
Her feet and hands were skin and bones.

Always thinking at home
Made Zhu Niu sick.
But to find a good place
Would take some effort.

Zhu Niu got up
And walked into the deep mountain.
She searched from south to north,
And from east to west.

A little squirrel appeared
With a chestnut in its mouth.
Zhu Niu chased the squirrel
For seven hundred li①.

---

①　A unit of length, equivalent to 500 meters or half of a kilometer.

松鼠跑得快，
竺妞追得急。
追到黄土坡，
板栗落下地。

忽然一阵风，
松鼠无踪迹。
竺妞找板栗，
板栗埋土里。

板栗发了芽，
长得高又大。
过了整三年，
栗子满树挂。

能长板栗树，
定能长庄稼。
这里土最肥，
竺妞笑哈哈。

松鼠来指点，
土坡开成田。
就从这时起，
天下有了田。

地在哪里开？
哪个来指点？

The squirrel ran fast,

And Zhu Niu chased hurriedly.

When they got to the loess slope,

The chestnut fell to the ground.

A sudden gust of wind came,

And the squirrel disappeared.

Zhu Niu looked for the chestnut,

Which was now buried in the dirt.

The chestnut sprouted,

And then grew tall and big.

After exactly three years,

Chestnuts were hanging all over the tree.

If a chestnut tree could grow here,

Crops surely could, too.

Having found the most fertile soil,

Zhu Niu smiled.

The squirrel came to guide

To turn the loess slope into the farmland.

From that moment on,

The world has had farmlands.

Where else to find the field?

Who could provide guidance?

竺妞又去找，
不怕路遥远！

一只小箐鸡，
嘴里含草籽。
竺妞追箐鸡，
追了七百里。

箐鸡飞得快，
竺妞追得急。
追到石旮旯，
草籽落下地。

忽然一阵风，
箐鸡无踪迹。
竺妞找草籽，
草籽埋土里。

草籽发了芽，
草藤满地爬。
过了三个月，
藤上开了花。

石缝长草棵，
定能长庄稼。

Zhu Niu went to seek again,

Fearless of the long distances!

A small Jingji① appeared,

With grass seeds in its mouth.

Zhu Niu chased it,

For seven hundred li.

Jingji ran fast,

And Zhu Niu chased hurriedly.

When they got to a stony corner,

The grass seeds fell to the ground.

A sudden gust of wind came,

And the Jingji disappeared.

Zhu Niu looked for the grass seeds,

Which were now in the dirt.

The grass seeds sprouted,

Its vines crawling all over the ground.

Three months later,

Flowers bloomed on the vines.

If grass could grow in the stony crevices,

Crops surely could, too.

---

① A kind of bird growing in bamboo forests.

这里土最肥，
竺妞笑哈哈。

箐鸡来指点，
石山劈成地。
就从这时起，
天下有了地。

松鼠和箐鸡，
有情又有意。
它们来指点，
开了田和地。

土坡咋个开？
石山怎样劈？
看看竺妞仙，
怎样出大力。

土坡高又陡，
上下很费力，
爬上又滑下，
跌破嘴和鼻。

竺妞穿草鞋，
披起麻蓑衣，
站在半天云，
挥锄不歇气。

Having found the most fertile soil,
Zhu Niu smiled.

With the guidance from the Jingji,
Stony mountains were halved into the field.
From that moment on,
The world has had the field.

The squirrel and Jingji
Were affectionate and warmhearted.
With their guidance,
Farmlands and fields were cultivated.

How to cultivate the loess slope?
How to halve the stony mountain?
Look at goddess Zhu Niu,
Who worked hard.

The slope was high and steep,
Making it hard to get up and down,
And she climbed up and slid down,
Bruising her mouth and nose.

Zhu Niu wore straw sandals,
Put on the raincoat of hemp,
Was high up in the clouds,
And hoed without a break.

一锄削坡头，
二锄填坡底，
三锄垒田埂，
四锄碎土坯。

垒好丘丘田，
又来开沟渠。
引来天河水，
灌在大田里。

田水绿汪汪，
好像块块玉。
竺妞开好田，
她又来开地。

石山硬邦邦，
怪石冲天立。
石尖像虎牙，
石笋如龙须。

竺妞挥金斧，
劈石来开地。
斧头落下来，
火星洒满地。

一斧劈石尖，
二斧破石壁，

She firstly hoed the slope leveled,
Secondly hoed the slope-bottom filled,
Thirdly hoed the ridges in the fields up,
And lastly hoed the soil lumps crumbled.

After building the hilly fields,
She opened the ditches.
The water from the river of heaven,
Was led to irrigate the farmland.

The farmlands with water were green
Like pieces of jade.
After Zhu Niu made the farmland
Before she came to make the field.

The stony mountain was hard
With strange rocks reaching to the sky.
The stony tips were like tigers' teeth,
And the stony spikes, dragons' beards.

Zhu Niu waved a gold axe,
And split the rocks to make the field.
When the axe hit,
Fiery sparks covered the ground.

She firstly axed the stony tip off,
Secondly axed the stony wall cracked,

苗族古歌 Ancient Miao Songs

三斧断石笋，
四斧除石基。

石尖投山南，
石壁丢河西，
石笋甩天涯，
石基坠海底。

怪石全除尽，
现出油黑泥。
再来捶泥团，
土像面样细。

坡田一台台，
伸到云彩里。
田水生蚂蟥，
田埂长田鸡。

平地一片片，
从东铺到西。
地头生土蚕，
地脚长蛐蛐。

蚂蟥和田鸡，
土蚕和蛐蛐，
一起来祝贺：
有了田和地！

Thirdly axed the stony spikes broken.
And lastly axed the stony foundation loose.

With the stony tips hurled to the south,
Stony walls tossed to the west of the river,
The stony spikes, flung to the horizon,
The stony foundation sank to the seafloor.

With all strange rocks removed,
The shiny black mud appeared.
The mud was kneaded into balls,
As fine as doughs of flour.

Farmlands on the slopes of the mountains
Were like steps reached into the clouds.
While the water in the farmland bred leeches,
Frogs populated the ridges in the farmland.

Patches of the flat fields
Stretched from east to west.
Silkworms grew at the head of the field,
And crickets grew at the foot of it.

Leeches and frogs,
Silkworms and crickets,
Came together to celebrate:
There were now farmlands and fields!

二、造牛

有了田和地，
水牛没一只，
黄牛没一头，
哪样犁田地？

喊狗来犁田，
叫马来犁地。
马来驾弯担，
狗来拖木犁。

马的肩膀滑，
弯担驾不起；
狗的脚杆细，
下田不得力。

马也靠不住，
狗也不成器。
到底要哪样，
来犁田和地？

竺妞大神仙，
她来驾弯担；
竺妞大神仙，
她来拖木犁。

Section 2　Cattle Making

Now there were farmlands and fields,
But no buffalo,
And no ox,
So who would plow the farmland and the field?

The dog was called to plow the farmland,
And the horse, to plow the field.
The horse tried to carry the pole,
And the dog, pull the wood plow.

The horse's shoulders were too sloped
To carry the pole;
The dog's limbs were too skinny
To work in the farmland.

The horse could not be relied on,
Nor could the dog.
Who was suitable
For plowing the farmland and the field?

The great goddess Zhu Niu,
She herself came to carry the pole.
The great goddess Zhu Niu,
She herself came to pull the wood plow.

竺妞来犁田，
竺妞来犁地。
从早犁到晚，
一天不歇气。

喘气像吹风，
淌汗像落雨，
满脸湿漉漉，
浑身都是泥。

腰杆软瘫瘫，
爬也爬不起；
肩膀血淋淋，
烂肉又烂皮。

不吃饭一颗，
不喝水一滴，
躺在床上哼，
吁吁自叹息：

"我的皮肉嫩，
怎能来拖犁？
还是要牯牛，
才能犁田地！"

哪个来造牛？
竺妞造黄牛，

Zhu Niu came to plow the farmland,
And the field.
Plowing from morning till night,
She didn't rest for a day.

She breathed like the wind blowing,
Sweated like the rain falling,
Her face becoming wet,
Her whole body being covered with mud.

Her waist was so sore
That she could not stand up anymore.
Her shoulders were bleeding,
Bruised and raw.

Not eating a grain of rice,
Or drinking a drop of water,
She lay in bed groaning,
Palpitating and sighing:

"How can my tender body
Plow the field?
It still has to be the oxen
To plow the field!"

Who would make the oxen?
Zhu Niu made them,

竺妞造水牛,
天下有了牛。

咋个造黄牛?
黄泥捏黄牛。
咋个造水牛?
黑泥捏水牛。

黄牛捏好了,
放在黄土坡。
竺妞吹口气,
黄牛叫哞哞。

水牛捏好了,
放在大河边。
竺妞吹口气,
水牛叫昂昂。

黄牛叫哞哞,
水牛叫昂昂,
甩起四条腿,
蹦蹦来撒欢。

黄牛要斗架,
两角向前弯;
水牛要凫水,
两角向后弯。

and the buffaloes,

The world has had cattle from then on.

How did she make the oxen?

She molded them with yellow mud.

How did she make the buffaloes?

She molded them with black mud.

The molded oxen

Were placed on the loess slope.

When Zhu Niu breathed into them,

The oxen mooed.

The molded buffaloes

Were placed by the big river.

When Zhu Niu breathed into them,

The buffaloes bellowed.

The mooing oxen,

The bellowing buffaloes,

Swiped their four legs,

Prancing and frolicking.

When the oxen fought,

They charged their horns forward;

When the buffaloes swam,

They bent their horns backward.

水牛来犁田，
黄牛来犁地。
田里种谷子，
地里种玉麦。

谷子一串串，
哪个来传种？
玉麦一包包，
哪个来传种？

三、找种子

竺妞找种子，
过了九个岭；
竺妞找种子，
翻了九道箐。

忽然有一天，
竺妞过松林。
松鼠吱吱叫，
竺妞仔细听：

"要找谷子种，
等我肚子疼。
肚子拉了稀，
就有谷子种。"

松鼠说得清，

The buffaloes plowed the farmlands,

And the oxen plowed the fields.

Millets were planted in the farmlands,

And corns, in the fields.

Ears of millets,

Where would the seeds be found?

Ears of corns,

Where would the seeds be found?

Section 3   Seeds Seeking

Zhu Niu went to look for seeds,

And she crossed nine ridges;

Zhu Niu went to look for seeds,

And she crossed nine valleys.

Suddenly one day,

Zhu Niu came upon a pine forest.

A squirrel was squeaking,

So Zhu Niu listened carefully:

"If you want to look for millet seeds,

Wait till my stomach hurts.

When I poop,

You will have millet seeds."

The squirrel's words were very clear,

竺妞听得真。
松鼠去找食，
竺妞坐起等。

等了七百天，
松鼠回松林。
竺妞问松鼠：
"肚子疼不疼？"

"再等七百天，
肚子才会疼。
要是等不得，
种子难找寻！"

"为了找种子，
不怕日子长。
别说七百天，
千年也等得！"

松鼠去找食，
找到昆南山。
找了多少天？
刚好七百天。

松鼠回松林，
就喊肚子疼。
疼得忍不住，
躺下就打滚。

And Zhu Niu listened attentively.
When the squirrel went to look for food,
Zhu Niu sat and waited.

After she waited for seven hundred days,
The squirrel came back to the pine forest.
Zhu Niu asked the squirrel:
"Does your stomach hurt?"

"Another seven hundred days will pass,
Before my stomach hurts.
If you can't wait,
It will be hard for you to find the seeds!"

"In order to find the seeds,
The long wait is nothing.
To say nothing of seven hundred days,
A thousand years will be waited out!"

The squirrel went to find food
In the Kunnan Mountain.
How many days did it take?
It was exactly seven hundred days.

When it returned to the pine forest,
The squarrel cried that its stomach hurt.
The pain was so unbearable
That it rolled on the ground.

松鼠拉稀屎，
屙出七颗谷。
谷子没消化，
颗颗圆鼓鼓。

竺妞捧起谷，
感谢小松鼠。
谷子搬进田，
芽芽就冒出。

谷子出了穗，
一串挨一串。
到底为哪样，
穗子长成串？

你看那松鼠，
尾巴蓬松松。
就是这尾巴，
变成谷穗穗。

找到谷子种，
又找玉麦种。
竺妞进深箐，
箐鸡叫咕咕：

"要找玉麦种，
等我把血吐。

In the squirrel's runny stool
Were seven grains of millet.
The millet had not been digested,
So they were round and full.

Zhu Niu picked up the grains
And thanked the little squirrel.
When the grains were sown in the farmland,
The sprouts burgeoned.

The millets grew ears,
One after another.
How did,
Those ears of grains appear?

Look at the squirrel,
The tail of which was fluffy.
It was this tail that turned into
Ears of grains.

The millet seeds had been found,
And next were the seeds of the corn.
Zhu Niu went to the deep bamboo forest,
Where a Jingji was clucking:

"If you want to find the corn seeds,
Wait till I spit blood.

嗉子出了血，
种子就吐出。"

箐鸡去找食，
找到昆南山。
竺妞坐起等，
等了七百天。

箐鸡飞回来，
嗉子胀得大，
像个大葫芦，
挂在脖子下。

箐鸡张开口，
吐出七口血。
七颗玉麦种，
一起吐出来。

捧起玉麦种，
竺妞心喜欢。
赶紧带回来，
撒在地中间。

种子冒了芽，
七天就长高。
冒出红须须，
背起青苞苞。

When my crop bleeds,
I will spit out the seeds."

The Jingji went to find food
In the Kunnan Mountain.
Zhu Niu sat and waited,
For seven hundred days.

When the Jingji flew back,
Its crop was swollen,
Like a big gourd,
Hanging under its neck.

The Jingji opened its mouth
And spit blood seven times.
Seven corn seeds
Were spit out all at once.

Picking up the corn seeds,
Zhu Niu was very glad.
She brought them back quickly,
And spread them in the field.

The seeds sprouted,
And grew tall in seven days.
They developed red tassels
And green corncobs.

到底为哪样，
须须红彤彤？
那是箐鸡血，
把它来染红。

Why

The tassels are red?

That was the Jingji's blood,

That dyed them red.

第四章　婚事

一、留姑娘

远古的时候，
山中的雀鸟。
哪个会下蛋？
哪个来抱蛋？

远古的时候，
人类的婚姻，
哪个嫁出去？
哪个留下来？

远古的时候，
山中的雀鸟，
公的会下蛋，
母的来抱蛋。

远古的时候，
人类的婚姻，

Chapter 4　Marriage

Section 1　Daughters Staying at Home

A long, long time ago,

Of the birds in the mountains,

Which ones could lay eggs?

Which ones would hatch them?

A long, long time ago,

In human marriage,

Who left the home when getting married?

Who stayed with the parents?

A long, long time ago,

Of the birds in the mountains,

The cocks could lay eggs,

And the hens hatched them.

A long, long time ago,

In human marriage,

儿子嫁出去，
姑娘留下来。

儿子长大了，
长出好模样。
姑娘就来选，
讨他做新郎。

姑娘不出嫁，
留下管家常。
大小家务事，
姑娘拿主张。

儿子嫁出去，
不到一周年。
爹妈的房子，
垮了十二间。

风来挡不了，
雨来没遮拦。
日子不好过，
生活多艰难。

儿子嫁出去，
不到九个月。
爹妈的房子，
坏了十二格。

Sons left the home when getting married,
And daughters stayed with the parents.

When a son grew up,
Grew into a handsome young man,
Girls then came,
Each courting him to be her groom.

Daughters did not leave their family,
And stayed to manage household affairs.
All affairs big and small,
Were decided by these daughters.

The son left on getting married
For less than one year.
His parents' house
Had twelve rooms collapsed.

The house no long shielded the wind,
Or shelter them from the rain.
Days did not pass easily,
And life became hard.

The son left on getting married
For less than nine months.
His parents' house
Had twelve places damaged.

霜来遮不了，
雪来挡不住。
生活多困苦，
日子没法度。

爹妈的房子，
倒了十二间。
坐在堂屋里，
抬头看见天。

久久没人修，
小雨下来了，
阿妈拿锄头，
在家挖小沟。

爹妈的房子，
坏了十二格，
坐在房间里，
可以望银河。

久久没人补，
大雨下来了，
阿爹忙抬土，
在家四处堵。

房倒等着搭，
房塌等着撑。

The house no longer kept out the frost
Or the snow.
Life was hard,
And days passed with difficulty.

His parents' house,
Had twelve rooms collapsed.
Sitting in the living room,
One could see the sky.

With the house in disrepair for a long time,
When the light rain came,
The mother would take a hoe
To dig small ditches in the house.

The parents' house
Had twelve places damaged.
Sitting in the bedrooms,
One could see the Milky Way.

With the house in disrepair for a long time,
When the heavy rain came,
The father would hurry to use dirt
To stop the water from flooding the house.

The collapsed house was waiting for rebuilding,
And damaged parts, waiting for repairing.

阿妈上街去，
买回一把锛。

房烂等着修，
房破等着补。
阿爹上街去，
买来一把斧。

劈树有了锛，
砍树有了斧。
有了锛和斧，
爹妈仍叫苦：

"谁人来用锛？
哪个来使斧？
谁人来捆树？
哪个来扛树？"

大姑娘用锛，
二姑娘用斧，
三姑娘捆树，
四姑娘扛树。

姑娘一大群，
上山登路程。
唱唱又笑笑，
四处是歌声。

The mother went out
And bought an adze.

The dilapidated house was waiting for repairing,
And the holes, waiting for fixing.
The father went out
And bought an axe.

There were now the adze to split the trees
And axe to cut them down.
But with both the adze and the axe,
The parents were still worried:

"Who can use the adze?
Who can use the axe?
Who can bundle the trees?
Who can carry them?"

The eldest daughter would try the adze,
The second daughter, the axe,
The third daughter, the tree bundling,
And the fourth daughter, the tree carrying.

A large group of the daughters,
Went up the mountain.
They sang and laughed,
The songs resonating in the air.

姑娘笑声脆，
唱歌也好听。
要是绣裙子，
会使绣花针。

谁说姑娘傻？
谁说姑娘笨？
姑娘手灵巧，
自古出了名！

可是来砍树，
双手就不灵。
锛也不会用，
斧也使不成。

捆也不会捆，
扛也扛不动。
用尽平生力，
累得打哼哼。

砍棵大松树，
高有十二丈，
粗有十二围，
哼着砍七天。

四个来四方，
八个来八面。

Their laughters were crisp,

And they sang well.

If they embroidered skirts,

they could use embroidery needles.

Who says girls are silly?

Who says girls are slow?

Their dexterous hands

Have been famous since ancient times!

But when it came to felling trees,

Their hands were not as able.

They could not use the adze

Or the axe.

They did not know how to bundle,

Nor were they strong enough to carry.

They used all their strength

But only moaned with tiredness.

Trying to fell a big pine tree,

That was twelve zhang tall,

And twelve wei① thick,

They tried and moaned for seven days.

Four of them came from four sides,

And eight of them, from eight directions.

---

① An arm-span (what one can hold with both two arms stretched).

大家一起来，
叫着捆八天。

八个来八方，
四个来四面。
大家一起来，
哭着扛九天。

哼也哼够了，
叫也叫累了，
哭也哭饱了，
树还不到家！

爹妈的房子，
倒了没人修；
爹妈的房子，
坏了没人补。

消息传开去，
儿子很着急。
赶忙跑回家，
开口问爹妈：

"阿爹和阿妈，
快快来回答，
房子怎么坏？
房子咋个垮？

All of them came together,

Yelling as they bundled for eight days.

They came from eight directions,

And from four sides.

All of them came,

Crying as they tried to carry for nine days.

They were tired from moaning,

And yelling,

Satiated with tears,

But the trees had not come home yet!

The parents' house

Was falling but no one could fix it;

The parents' house

Was damaged but no one could repair it.

The news spread,

And the son was worried.

He hurried home

And asked his parents:

"Mom and Dad,

Please tell me quickly,

How was the house damaged?

How did the collapse happen?

"阿姐和阿妹，
怎么不在家？
我要叫她们，
修房帮爹妈！"

阿爹和阿妈，
一起来回答：
"自从你出嫁，
房子坏又垮。

"阿姐和阿妹，
砍树离开家。
她们扛不动，
至今没归家。"

儿子听了话，
心急如猫抓。
取下身上弩，
就往墙上挂。

提锛又背斧，
急忙进山洼。
儿子会砍树，
斧声响嗒嗒。

一棵大松树，
只是砍七斧，

"Where are my sisters,

And why are they not at home?

I'm going to ask them,

To help you repair the house! "

The parents

Answered in one voice:

"Ever since you got married and left,

The house has been deteriorating.

"Your sisters

Have left home to fell the trees.

They are unable to carry them

And have not come back home."

On hearing this, the son

Felt anxious as if a cat were scratching at his heart.

He unloaded the crossbow from himself

And hung it on the wall.

He picked up the adze, carried the axe,

And hurried into the valley.

The son was good at felling trees,

The axe clattering.

A big pine tree,

With just seven strikes,

倒在大路边，
两头一样粗。

像根直麻秆，
正好做大柱。
只有靠儿子，
才能修房屋。

一棵大杉树，
只是砍八斧，
倒在水沟旁，
头细根根粗。

像根长竹竿，
正好做二柱。
只有靠儿子，
房子才能补。

松树扛回来，
不费啥力气；
杉树扛回来，
不费啥工夫。

把它放上肩，
抬脚就走路。
跨沟不用搀，
跳坎不用扶。

Fell by the side of the road,
Both ends of equal thickness.

Like a straight hemp stalk,
It was just right for the grand pillar.
Only by relying on the son,
Could the parents' house be repaired.

A big fir tree,
With just eight strikes,
Fell down by the ditch,
The head thinner than the root.

Like a long bamboo pole,
It was just right for the second pillar.
Only by relying on the son,
Could the parents' house be repaired.

The pine tree was carried back
Without causing him much trouble;
The fir tree was carried back
Without taking him much time.

Putting them on his shoulder,
He set off right away.
He didn't need any help when crossing the ditches,
Or support when stepping over the ridges.

早上立大柱，
晌午立二柱。
挨晚上椽子，
黄昏将草铺。

房子修好了，
房子补好了。
阿妈喜欢了，
阿爹说话了：

"儿子要留下，
儿子不能嫁。
把他留在家，
盖房种庄稼。"

"姑娘嫁出去，
别人讨了她，
做个好媳妇，
纺麻又绣花。"

人类的婚姻，
从此有变化。
家中有女儿，
长大就出嫁。

儿子长大了，
媳妇讨进家，
生儿又育女，
侍奉爹和妈。

He set up the grand pillar in the morning,
And the second pillar at noon.
He installed the rafters by late afternoon
And thatched the roof by dusk.

The house was repaired
And was patched.
The mother was happy,
And the father said:

"The son should be kept at home,
Cannot leave on getting married.
He should be kept at home,
To build the house and grow crops."

"The daughter goes to the in-laws,
To marry into that family,
To be a good daughter-in-law,
To spin, weave and embroider."

The human marriage
Has changed ever since then.
Daughters in each family
Live with the in-laws on getting married.

When the sons grow up,
They marry their wives into the family,
Having their own children,
And looking after their parents.

二、嫁姑娘

远古的时候，
山中的雀鸟，
公的会下蛋，
母的来抱蛋。

远古的时候，
人类的婚姻，
儿子嫁出去，
姑娘留下来。

留下做哪样？
留下讨新郎。
留下做哪样？
留下管家常。

绣花纺麻线，
织裙裁衣裳。
姑娘手灵巧，
样样都停当。

可是盖房子，
姑娘没主张。
地基不会挖，
木料不会扛。

Section 2 Daughters Marrying out of Home

A long, long time ago,
Of the birds in the mountains,
The cocks could lay eggs,
And the hens hatched them.

A long, long time ago,
In human marriages,
Sons went to live with the in-laws,
While daughters stayed at home.

What did they do when they stayed?
They married their grooms into the family.
What did they do when they stayed?
They stayed to deal with household affairs.

They spun, weaved and embroidered,
Knitted skirts and made clothes.
They had dexterous hands
That did everything well.

But when it came to building houses,
They didn't know what to do.
They could not dig for the foundation
Or carry the lumber.

柱子立不起，
椽子搭不上，
不会铺茅草，
不会垒泥墙。

再说种庄稼，
姑娘也没法。
不会挑粪草，
不会犁和耙。

种子撒下地，
多久不发芽。
就是发了芽，
也很难开花。

又说放牛羊，
姑娘更为难。
路远难得走，
山高不好攀。

牛瘦羊儿小，
瘪得像扁担，
几根光骨头，
毛长屁股尖。

要想住新房，
想得心发痒；
要想吃白米，
想得口水淌。

They could not erect the pillars
Or install the rafters.
They could not lay thatches
Or build mud walls.

About growing crops,
They did not know it either.
They could not carry the grass compost,
Or plow or rake the field.

The seeds they sowed
Did not germinate for a long time.
Even when the seeds did sprout,
They hardly ever bloomed.

About herding the livestock,
They had an even harder time.
It was a long distance,
And the mountains were too high.

The cattle were thin and the sheep were small,
Shrivelled like the shoulder poles,
With nothing but skins and bones,
And long hair and skinny hips.

They wanted to live in a new house,
With pining hearts;
They wanted to eat white rice,
With watering mouths.

要想吃牛羊，
瘦骨熬清汤。
爹妈干着急，
只怪留姑娘。

阿爹改了心，
阿妈变了意。
儿子留下来，
姑娘嫁出去。

儿子管家常，
样样都在行。
盖房种庄稼，
又会放牛羊。

新房盖得高，
庄稼长得旺，
牛儿长得肥，
羊儿长得胖。

蜜蜂长旺了，
它就会分家；
姑娘长大了，
就要她出嫁。

姑娘几时嫁，
初一初二嫁。
小伴三四个，
一起来送她。

They wanted to eat beef and mutton
But only got clear soup with lean bones.
The parents were anxious,
Regretting they kept the daughters home.

The father had a change of heart,
And the mother had a change of mind.
The son would stay at home,
And daughters, leave on getting married.

The son running the home affairs
Was good at everything.
He could build houses, grow crops,
And herd cattle and sheep.

The new house was built high,
And the crops grew vigorously,
The cattle were stout,
And the sheep were fat.

When bees thrive,
They split up;
When daughters grow up,
They leave home to be married.

The auspicious day for daughters to marry
Was the first or the second day of the month.
Three or four of her friends,
Came to accompany her.

阿爹拿口袋，
装了荞粑粑，
递给亲女儿，
眼里闪泪花：

"爹的女儿呀，
今天你出嫁。
路上肚子饿，
你就吃粑粑。"

阿妈拿把伞，
心里乱如麻。
递给亲女儿，
说起知心话：

"妈的女儿呀，
今天你出嫁。
路上太阳辣，
你就把伞打。"

姑娘接口袋，
不说一句话。
望了爹一眼，
就把泪水擦。

姑娘接了伞，
不说一句话。
望了妈一眼，
低头扭手帕。

The father took a pouch,
Filled with buckwheat pancakes,
And gave it to the daughter,
Tears sparkling in his eyes:

"My dear daughter,
Today you leave to get married.
If you are hungry on the way,
Eat these pancakes."

The mother took an umbrella,
With a heavy heart.
Handing the embrella to her daughter,
She said words from her heart:

"My dear daughter,
Today you leave to get married.
The sun is scorching on the way,
So use this umbrella."

The daughter took the pouch
Without saying a word.
She looked at her father,
Wiping away her tears.

The girl took the umbrella
Without saying a word.
She looked at her mother,
Lowering her head and twisting the kerchief.

爹对姑娘说：
"爹的女儿呀，
你要放宽心，
好好去公家。"

"早晚敬阿公，
递烟又端茶。
三百六十天，
要听阿公话。"

"我在房子边，
栽上一棵麻，
等麻长高了，
接你来织麻。"

妈对姑娘说：
"妈的女儿呀，
心里莫难过，
好好去婆家。"

"早晚敬阿婆，
像待亲阿妈。
煮饭不要硬，
炒菜不要辣。"

"我在园子里，
种上一棵花，
等花开艳了，
接你来绣花。"

The father said to her:
"My dear daughter,
You need not worry,
Just go to the house of your father-in-law."

"Greet him each morning and night,
And serve him his pipe and tea.
Each of the three hundred and sixty days,
Listen to your father-in-law."

"By our house I will grow
A hemp plant,
Which will grow tall when
I will get you back to weave with it."

The mother said:
"My dear daughter,
Don't feel sad,
Just go to the house of your mother-in-law."

"Greet her each morning and night,
Treating her like you treat me.
Do not cook the rice half-done,
And do not cook dishes too spicy."

"In our garden I will,
Plant a flowery plant,
Which will bloom when,
I will get you back for embroidery."

哥哥对妹说：
"今天妹出嫁，
只管放心去，
一点莫牵挂。"

"家里有我在，
服侍爹和妈。
砍树盖房子，
犁地种庄稼。"

"我在山梁上，
搭间小草房。
四面编竹篱，
有门又有窗。"

"支条小板凳，
摆张小木床。
妹妹来回走，
歇脚躲阴凉。"

哥的一番话，
说得妹伤心。
今日相别离，
哥妹情意深。

树大要分桠，
妹大要嫁人。
心中虽难舍，
还是要离分。

The brother said to his sister:
"Today when you leave to get married,
Just go without no worries
About anything."

"I am at home
To attend to our father and mother.
I can fell trees for building houses
And plow the field for growing crops."

"On the mountain ridge I will build
A small straw house.
Enclosed with weaved bamboo fences,
It will have doors and windows."

"I will put a small bench inside,
And set up a small wooden bed.
When you travel back and forth,
You can rest in the house."

The brother's words
Moved the sister.
They parted ways on that day,
With deep brother-sister affection.

Like big trees branching out,
Grown daughters would leave to marry.
Although it was hard,
She still had to depart.

四个小伙伴，
一起送妹行。
爬坡又上坎，
翻山又过林。

走到山梁上，
汗水湿衣襟，
坐下歇个脚，
扇风定定神。

吃块荞粑粑，
粑粑甜津津；
喝口山泉水，
泉水凉阴阴。

拿出小木梳，
拿出小铜镜。
对镜整整容，
又来赶路程。

来到新郎家，
老少来欢迎。
郎家摆酒宴，
亲友满门庭。

磕头拜天地，
端酒敬亲人。
新郎和新娘，
合意又同心。

Four of her friends,
Came to accompany her.
They climbed hills and ridges,
Crossed mountains and forests.

When they walked up the ridge,
They were sweating,
So they sat down to have a rest,
Fanning to calm their minds.

They ate the buckwheat pancakes,
Which were pleasantly sweet;
They drank the mountain spring water,
Which was delightfully cool.

The bride took out a small wooden comb
And a small copper mirror.
Having made sure she looked nice,
She continued her journey.

When they arrived at the groom's home,
Everyone old and young welcomed them.
The groom's family hosted a banquet,
Relatives and friends filling the courtyard.

Having thanked heaven and earth,
The bride and groom made toasts to all.
The two of them
Were a good match and thought alike.

哪个是公婆，
新娘要去认；
哪个是姑嫂，
新娘要去认。

家门和族内，
个个要认清；
三朋和四友，
个个要认准。

出嫁整三天，
就要去回门。
新郎和新娘，
双双转回程。

阿爹忙摆酒，
阿妈忙点灯。
新郎忙磕头，
诚心拜神灵。

哥哥来相见，
妹夫可英俊？
新郎好人品，
一家都称心。

桃子开了花，
也就要结果；
南瓜熟透了，
瓜蒂就脱落。

The groom's father and mother,
The bride went to see;
The sisters-in-law,
The bride went to visit.

All relatives on groom's side,
The bride needed to know;
All friends of groom's family,
The bride needed to remember.

Three days after the wedding,
They must visit the bride's family.
The groom and bride together
Journeyed back to the bride's family.

The bride's father offered the wine,
While the mother lit the lamps.
The groom kowtowed
To thank the gods sincerely.

The bride's brother came,
Was the brother-in-law handsome?
The groom had a fine character,
Satisfying the whole family.

Once the peach tree blooms,
Peaches are borne;
Once the pumpkin is ripe,
The pedicel breaks off.

苗族古歌 Ancient Miao Songs

姑娘来出嫁，
一晃半年多。
过冬坐了月，
杀狗来庆贺。

姑娘吃狗肉，
舒筋又活络，
娃娃长得胖，
全家笑呵呵！

The daughter's married life,

Flew by quickly for more than half a year.

In her postbirth confinement in the winter,

A dog was butchered to celebrate.

The new mother ate the dog meat

To help with her muscles and joints,

To keep the baby healthy,

And to make the whole family happy!

第五章　丧葬

一、生死

山中的树木，
为啥会落叶？
世上的人类，
为啥会死去？

山中的树木，
秋天就落叶；
世上的人类，
老了就会死。

远古的时候，
人死怎么办？
不用棺材装，
不兴埋深山。

人刚断了气，
亲属泪涟涟，
响箭射三支，
四方阴惨惨。

Chapter 5 Funeral

Section 1 Life and Death

Why do trees in the mountains
Shed leaves?
Why do humans in the world
Pass away?

Trees in the mountains
Shed leaves in the fall;
Humans in the world
Pass away in old age.

A long, long time ago,
What did they do when people died?
They didn't use coffins
Or bury the dead in deep mountains.

As soon as they breathed their last breath,
The relatives in tears,
Shot three whistling arrows,
Into the gloom within the four directions.

173

响箭来报丧，
满寨人听见，
来到死者家，
围在尸体前。

天神来规定，
死人要吃完。
不能留一块，
不得留一片。

天神的规定，
世代来相传，
传到子耿家，
这才断了线。

子耿性耿直，
子耿心最好，
上山去打猎，
养活亲阿妈。

打得小野鸡，
就先敬阿妈。
羊儿跟娘走，
子耿不离妈。

忽然有一天，
阿妈老病发。
水也不能喝，
饭也吃不下。

The whistling arrows sent the sad news
To people in the village,
Who then came to the deceased's house,
Making a circle around the dead.

The god of heaven dictated,
The corpse must be eaten up.
Not one piece should be spared,
Not one slice.

The dictate of the god of heaven
Was passed on for generations,
Until the house of Zi Geng,
That finally abandoned this practice.

Zi Geng was upright in nature,
Had the kindest heart,
And relied on hunting in the mountains,
To support his mother.

When he hunted a little pheasant,
He would give his mother to eat first.
Like lambs who followed their mothers,
Zi Geng never left his mother.

Suddenly one day,
His mother's chronic disease worsened.
She could not drink water
Or eat anything.

子耿流着泪，
设法救阿妈。
早上请巫师，
晚上求白马。

巫师来问神，
白马来卜卦，
一天闹到晚，
忙得眼不眨。

巫师来七回，
白马来七遍。
阿妈的病情，
一点也不减。

过了两三天，
阿妈闭了眼。
子耿连声叫，
子耿放声喊。

阿妈不答应，
不再睁开眼。
千呼和万唤，
总是听不见。

阿妈躺在床，
一动也不动。
四肢硬邦邦，
浑身冷冰冰。

Zi Geng with tears running down his face,
Tried to save his mother.
He implored the shaman in the morning,
Begged the white horse for help at night.

He had the shaman to implore the gods
And the white horse to tell the fortune,
So from morning till night,
He was too busy to close his eyes.

The shaman came seven times,
And the white horse, seven times.
But his mother's condition
Did not improve at all.

After two or three days,
His mother closed her eyes.
Zi Geng kept shouting
And calling her names.

His mother didn't respond,
Could no longer open her eyes.
He called again and again,
But she could no longer hear him.

His mother was lying in bed,
Not moving any more.
Her limbs turned stiff,
And her body, cold.

子耿俯下身，
搂着妈的颈，
号啕大声哭，
哭得多伤心！

子耿忙射箭，
响箭鸣三声。
寨中亲和友，
提刀就来临。

子耿见此景，
心中痛难忍：
"求求众乡亲，
听我说分明。"

他把好话讲：
"吃死人的肉，
是天神规定，
我们来改变。"

"邻友乡亲们，
我有事商量，
阿妈已去世，
大家要帮忙。"

"我来杀头牛，
再备酒七缸。
大家吃一台，
给妈来办丧。"

Zi Geng leaned over,
Holding his mother's neck,
Crying loudly,
His heart broken!

Zi Geng hurried to shoot arrows,
Three whistling arrows.
His relatives and friends in the village
Came with knives in their hands.

Seeing this,
Zi Geng felt unbearable pains in his heart:
"I beg all fellow villagers,
Please listen to my explanation."

He said kindly:
"Eating the flesh of the dead person,
Is dictated by the god of heaven,
But it is time we change it."

"My friends and fellow villagers,
I want to discuss with you,
That my mother has passed away,
And I need your help."

"I'll kill an ox,
And prepare seven vats of wine.
Let's have a feast,
And have a funeral for my mother."

"做个木盒子，
将妈尸体装，
送到山上去，
挖土来埋葬。"

子耿这番话，
感动众乡亲。
大家齐动手，
杀牛待客人。

吃过牛肉宴，
就来办事情。
砍树做木盒，
一会就做成。

阿妈盒里装，
抬到高山里。
挖土掩埋好，
砌成一座坟。

就从这时起，
不再吃死人。
死人装棺材，
杀牛祭天神。

二、芦笙和鼓

远古的时候，

"Let's make a wooden box
To put the body of my mother in,
Then carried it to the mountain
And bury it in the ground."

Zi Geng's words
Moved all the villagers.
Everyone gave a hand
To butcher the ox and treat the guests.

After the beef feast,
They started to work.
Cutting down trees for the wooden box,
They got it all done in no time.

His mother was laid into the box,
And carried to the high mountain.
They dug the pit, buried the box,
And built the grave mound.

From this moment on,
People no longer ate corpses.
As the dead would be put in the coffin,
Oxen, sacrificed for the god of heaven.

Section 2   Lu Sheng[①] and Drum

A long time ago,

---

① The reed-pipe wind instrument (used by the Miao, Yao and Dong ethnic groups).

苗族古歌 Ancient Miao Songs

天上热腾腾；
远古的时候，
地上光秃秃。

是谁来种树，
树才满山岭？
哪个来种竹，
竹才长成林？

竺妞来种树，
竺妞来种竹。
树木青葱葱，
竹子翠生生。

竹子长高了，
拿来做哪样？
树木长大了，
拿来做哪样？

竹子长高了，
拿来做芦笙；
树木长大了，
拿来做大鼓。

芦笙有啥用？
大鼓有啥用？
芦笙能传话，
大鼓能传声。

the sky was extremely hot;
A long time ago,
The earth was bare.

Who planted the trees,
That grew all over the mountains?
Who planted the bamboo,
That grew into a grove?

Zhu Niu planted the trees
And the bamboo.
The trees were green,
And the bamboo was verdant.

When the bamboo grew tall,
What could it be used for?
When the trees grew big,
What could they be used for?

When the bamboo grew tall,
They were used to make the Lu Sheng;
When the trees grew big,
They were used to make big drums.

What was the use of the Lu Sheng?
What was the use of the big drum?
The Lu Sheng could transmit messages,
And the big drum could transmit sound.

芦笙呜呜响，
吹出怀亲调；
大鼓咚咚敲，
赶来凑热闹。

芦笙传了话，
大鼓传了声。
亲戚和朋友，
才好悼亲人。

远古的时候，
大鼓是谁造？
远古的时候，
芦笙是谁造？

远古的时候，
人类还年轻。
不会造大鼓，
不会造芦笙。

不兴打大鼓，
也不吹芦笙。
家里死了人，
单靠箭传音。

没有啥音响，
没有令动静。
一家孤零零，
堂屋冷清清。

The Lu Sheng was played,
To remember the loved ones;
The drum was played,
To call people to get together.

The lu Sheng transmitted messages,
While the drum transmitted sound.
Relatives and friends,
knew to come to mourn the loved ones.

A long time ago,
Who made the big drum?
A long time ago,
Who made the Lu Sheng?

A long time ago,
The human race was still young.
People didn't know how to make the drum
Or the Lu Sheng.

They did not play the drum
Or the Lu Sheng.
When people passed away,
They used only arrows to spread the news.

There was hardly any sound
Or any movement.
The family was so lonely,
And the living room was quiet.

扎里和柏里，
同齐住一村。
村里死了人，
他俩最伤心。

柏里打主意：
"上天找竺妞，
向她借大鼓，
跟她借芦笙。"

"拿来办丧事，
村中闹腾腾。
死者得安慰，
生者也放心。"

扎里拍手说：
"这事我赞成，
你快准备好，
今天就动身！"

柏里上天去，
到了南天门。
当着竺妞面，
切切诉真情：

"借你大铜鼓，
借你金芦笙，
拿回地下去，
办丧好怀亲！"

Zha Li and Bo Li,
They lived in the same village.
When someone died in the village,
They two were the most wistful.

Bo Li thought of an idea:
"Go to see Zhu Niu in heaven,
To borrow the big drum
And the Lu Sheng from her."

"They can be used for the funeral
Giving a bustling atmosphere to the village.
The deceased will be consoled,
And the living will be at ease."

Zha Li clapped his hands and said:
"I agree to this,
So you get ready quickly
And take off today!"

Bo Li went up to heaven
And came to the Nantian Gate.
In front of Zhu Niu,
He told her the purpose of the visit:

"Please lend me your big bronze drum,
And your gold Lu Sheng,
So that I can take them back to earth
For holding funerals for the deceased!"

187

竺妞回答说：
"要借金芦笙，
要借大铜鼓，
我可不答应！"

柏里又说道：
"你的心最好，
你的情最真，
为何不答应？"

"芦笙只一把，
铜鼓只一个，
要是借给你，
我就用不成。"

"我只准许你，
瞧瞧金芦笙，
看看大铜鼓，
样子要记准。"

"回到地下去，
仿着造芦笙，
仿着造大鼓，
办丧祭亲人。"

"要是借给你，
你就造不成。
世上万万年，
没有鼓和笙。"

Zhu Niu replied：

"You want to borrow the gold Lu Sheng

And the bronze drum,

But I cannot let you do so！"

Bo Li said again：

"Your heart is the kindest,

And your affection is the most genuine,

But why don't you agree？"

"There being only one Lu Sheng

And only one bronze drum,

If I lend them to you,

I won't be able to use them."

"I will only let you

Look at the gold Lu Sheng

And the big bronze drum,

So do try to memorize their looks."

"When you go back to earth,

Make the Lu Sheng like mine

And make the big drum like mine

For holding funerals for the loved ones."

"If I lent them to you,

You would not learn to make them.

Then for eternity

The world will have no drum or Sheng."

苗族古歌 Ancient Miao Songs

"叫你仿着造,
学得好本领。
世上传大鼓,
人间传芦笙。"

柏里瞧瞧鼓,
又来看芦笙,
把它们模样,
牢牢记在心。

柏里不满足,
又把主意生:
又来学打鼓,
又学吹芦笙。

竺妞心最好,
竺妞情最真。
教他打大鼓,
教他吹芦笙。

柏里心最灵,
一下就学成。
竺妞很满意,
竺妞真高兴。

大鼓已瞧准,
芦笙已看清;
大鼓打得好,
芦笙吹得精。

190

"By making you use imitation,
I help you learn some good skills.
The world will have the big drum
And the Lu Sheng forever."

Bo Li looked at the drum
And then observed the Lu Sheng,
He memorized their appearances,
Firmly in his mind.

Bo Li was not satisfied
And thought of another idea:
He wanted to learn to play the drum
And the Lu Sheng.

Zhu Niu had the kindest heart
And the most genuine affection.
She taught him to play the drum
And the Lu Sheng.

Bo Li was the smartest,
And learned it in no time.
Zhu Niu was very satisfied,
And she was really happy.

The big drum was remembered firmly,
And the Lu Sheng was seen clearly;
The big drum was played well,
And the Lu Sheng was played wonderfully.

柏里回来了，
扎里来欢迎。
拉着柏里手，
细细问情况：

"这回上天去，
去借金芦笙，
去借大铜鼓，
竺妞可答应？"

"竺妞心最好，
竺妞情最真。
要借鼓和笙，
她却不答应。"

"既然心最好，
既然情最真，
要借鼓和笙，
为何不答应？"

"竺妞心最好，
竺妞情最真，
她要叫世上，
流传鼓和笙。"

"她来答应我，
瞧瞧金芦笙，
看看大铜鼓，
仿造鼓和笙。"

When Bo Li arrived back,
Zha Li came to greet him.
Holding Bo Li's hands,
He asked about the visit in detail:

"During your visit to heaven
To borrow the gold Lu Sheng
And the big bronze drum,
Did Zhu Niu agree to do so?"

"Zhu Niu has the kindest heart,
And the most genuine affection.
But to lend me the drum and the Lu Sheng,
She declined."

"If she has the kindest heart,
And the most genuine affection,
Why the plea to use the drum and Sheng,
Did she decline?"

"Zhu Niu has the kindest heart
And the most genuine affection.
She wants the world
To have drums and Shengs forever."

"She allowed me
To look at the gold Lu Sheng
And observe the big bronze drum
To make drums and Shengs like hers."

193

"竺妞心最好，
竺妞情最真。
听你这样说，
我也很开心。"

"要是借给我，
我就造不成。
世上万万年，
没有鼓和笙。"

"叫我仿着造，
学得好本领。
世上传大鼓，
人间传芦笙。"

"大鼓的样子，
你可记得清？
芦笙的模样，
你可记得准？"

"堂皇的大鼓，
你可造得成？
精致的芦笙，
你可削得成？

"响亮的大鼓，
你可敲得成？
动听的芦笙，
你可吹得成？"

"Zhu Niu has the kindest heart,
And the most genuine affection.
Having heard your explanation,
I am very glad, too."

"If she lent them to me,
I would not make them myself.
For eternity,
The world would have no drum or Sheng."

"Now that I must imitate what I saw,
I will learn good skills.
The world will have the big drum,
And the human race will have the Lu Sheng."

"What the big drum looks like,
Do you still remember clearly?
What the Lu Sheng looks like,
Do you still remember accurately?"

"The grand big drum,
Can you indeed make?
The exquisite Lu Sheng,
Can you indeed make?

"The booming drum,
Can you indeed play?
The melodious Lu Sheng,
Can you indeed play?"

"大鼓和芦笙，
模样都记清。
仿照样子造，
一定造得成！"

"我会敲大鼓，
我会吹芦笙。
敲得很响亮，
吹得很动听！"

"竺妞的芦笙，
本是金子造；
竺妞的大鼓，
本是铜铸成。"

"我们的芦笙，
哪样来制造？
我们的大鼓，
哪样来做成？"

"我们没有铜，
我们没有金。
砍树造大鼓，
砍竹制芦笙。"

柏里提起斧，
扎里拿起锛。
两人手拉手，
匆匆进山林。

"The big drum and the Lu Sheng,
I remember their looks clearly.
Imitating their looks,
I will surely succeed!"

"I know how to play the drum
And the Lu Sheng.
I can play the drum boomingly,
And the Lu Sheng, melodiously!"

"Zhu Niu's Lu Sheng
Was made of gold;
Zhu Niu's drum
Was molded out of copper."

"Our Lu Sheng,
What will it be made of?
Our big drum.
What will it be molded out of?"

"We have no copper,
And we have no gold either.
Let's cut trees to make the drum
And cut bamboo to make the Lu Sheng."

Bo Li took up an axe,
And Zha Li picked up an adze.
They two hand in hand
Hurried into the mountain forests.

砍下白木树，
修掉树枝枝，
锯掉树梢梢，
劈掉树根根。

中间留一截，
两端都削平。
刚有二尺长，
正好做鼓身。

砍下白竹子，
竹子亮晶晶，
中间钻孔孔，
正好做芦笙。

大鼓造好了，
芦笙也制成。
芦笙明晃晃，
大鼓圆滚滚。

大鼓和芦笙，
双双来配音。
好比夫和妻，
你响我来应。

丧事从此始，
打鼓吹芦笙。

They cut down a white birch,
Trimmed off its branches,
Saw off its treetops,
And chopped off its roots.

They kept the section in the middle,
And made both ends leveled.
It was exactly two chi① long,
Just right for the body of the drum.

They chopped down the white bamboo,
That was sparkling bright,
Drilled the holes in the middle,
Making the perfect Lu Sheng.

The big drum was completed,
And the Lu Sheng was also produced.
The Lu Sheng was bright,
And the drum was round.

The drum and the Lu Sheng
Accompanied each other
Like a couple,
Responding to each other.

At funerals from then on,
People have played the drum and the Lu Sheng.

---

① A traditional unit of length, equal to 1/3 meter.

谁家死了人。
鼓乐响不停。

大鼓敲三下，
响声震山岭。
亲戚和朋友，
忙来悼亲人。

芦笙吹三调，
声音响入云。
朋友和亲戚，
一起来送殡。

三、怀亲

孝子呀孝子，
话要这样说：
今天晚上呀，
叫你们起来！

看看母亲呀，
你们快起来！
你们不起来，
大家都悲哀。

明天一大早，
母亲要上山。
你们要留她，
她也不回来。

When a member of a family passed away,
The sound of drum and music never stops.

The drum sounded three times,
Shaking the hills and mountains.
Relatives and friends
Came quickly to mourn the loved one.

The Lu Sheng sounded three tones,
Ringing into the clouds.
Friends and relatives
Came quickly to attend the funeral.

Section 3 Keeping Vigils by Parents' Side

Filial children,
Let me tell you:
Tonight,
You must get up!

To see your mother for the last time,
Hurry and get up!
If you don't get up,
Everyone will be sad.

Early tomorrow morning,
Your mother will go up to the mountain.
No matter how much you want her to stay,
She will not return.

太阳升起来，
乌云来遮盖。
看也看不见，
心中可自在？

母亲上山去，
永远不回来。
你们到处找，
可会泪盈腮？

孝子呀孝子，
话要这样说：
今天晚上呀，
你们要起来！

看看爹爹呀，
你们快起来！
你们不起来，
这就不应该。

明天一早呀，
爹爹要上山。
你们要喊他，
他也不理睬。

月亮升起来，
黑云来遮盖。

When the sun is up,

Dark clouds can block it.

When you try but cannot see the sun,

Do you feel at ease?

Your mother will go up to the mountain,

And will never come back.

When you look for her everywhere,

Will your tears cover your face?

Filial children,

Let me tell you:

Tonight,

You must get up!

To see your father for the last time,

Hurry and get up.

If you don't get up,

You are wrong.

Early tomorrow morning,

Your father will go up to the mountain.

No matter how hard you call him back,

He will not respond to you.

When the moon is up,

The dark clouds can block it.

望也望不着，
心中不自在。

爹爹上山去，
永远不回来。
你们到处找，
就会泪满腮。

今晚机会好，
你们要起来，
起来看父母，
心中也痛快。

你们不起来，
不见父母面，
错过好机会，
悔恨千万代！

孝子呀孝子，
话要这样说：
今天晚上呀，
叫你们起来！

看看母亲呀，
你们快起来！
你们不起来，
真是发了呆！

When you try but cannot see the moon,
You will have the feeling of unease.

Your father will go up to the mountain,
And will never come back.
When you look for him everywhere,
Your tears will cover your face.

Tonight is a good opportunity,
So you must get up,
To see your parents
And to feel right.

If you do not get up,
Do not see your parents,
You will miss the good opportunity
And regret forever!

Filial children,
Let me tell you:
Tonight,
You must get up!

To see your mother,
Hurry and get up!
If you do not get up,
You are fools!

你们可知道？
你们出娘胎，
生在娘血里，
长在娘胸怀。

躺在娘腕里，
吃着娘的奶；
坐在娘腿上，
接受娘的爱。

想要小木梳，
娘就帮你买；
要想戴花朵，
娘就帮你戴。

要想穿裙子，
娘就帮你裁；
要想吃荞饭，
娘就帮你栽……

孝子呀孝子，
话要这样说：
今天晚上呀，
叫你们起来！

看看父亲呀，
你们快起来！

Do you know
That you came from her womb,
Were nourished by her blood,
And grew up in her bosom?

Lying in her arms,
You were fed by her milk;
Sitting on her laps,
You were attended to by her love.

When you wanted a small wooden comb,
She bought it for you;
When you wanted to wear flowers,
She did it for you.

When you wanted to wear a dress,
She tailored it for you;
When you wanted to eat buckwheat rice,
She cooked it for you...

Filial children,
Let me tell you:
Tonight,
You must get up!

To see your father for the last time,
Hurry and get up!

你们不起来，
时候就不在！

你们可知道？
你们小时候，
爹爹牵着你，
打猎上山来。

打着小鹌鹑，
问你爱不爱。
逮住小野兔，
叫你养起来。

鹌鹑你也爱，
野兔养起来。
爹爹又带你，
上山去砍柴。

搭个小凉棚，
把你遮起来；
不让狂风吹，
躲过太阳晒。

看见野果子，
伸手就去采。
采来递给你，
连声叫"乖乖"……

If you do not get up,
You will not get another chance to do so!

Do you know,
When you were little,
Your father took you by the hands,
To go hunting in the mountains?

Having hunted a small quail,
He asked if you liked it.
Having caught a little hare,
He let you raise it.

You liked the little quail
And raised the little hare.
Your father then took you
To the mountain to cut firewood.

He set up a little shed,
To shelter you from the elements;
It blocked the strong wind
And shaded the sun.

On seeing the wild berries,
He reached out to pick them for you.
Handing them to you,
He murmured over and over "little dear"...

孝子呀孝子，
话要这样说：
今天晚上呀，
叫你们起来！

看看父母呀，
你们快起来！
你们不起来，
画眉也悲哀。

父母的恩情，
真是深如海！
你们不遗忘，
就要快起来！

长者的话语，
句句都实在。
说到伤心处，
泪眼难睁开。

我要叫你们，
赶快爬起来，
见见父母面，
然后再跪拜。

父母的眉毛，
父母的眼睛，

Filial children,
Let me tell you:
Tonight,
You must get up!

To see your parents for the last time,
Hurry and get up!
If you do not get up,
Thrushes will also be sad.

The kindness of your parents
Is as deep as the sea!
If you have not forgotten,
Hurry and get up!

Words of the elders
Are honest and true.
They make you feel so sad,
Your tearful eyes could hardly open.

I must tell you
To get up quickly,
To see your parents,
And to kowtow to them.

Their eyebrows,
Their eyes,

父母的嘴角，
父母的脸腮；

父母的衣裙，
父母的腰带，
父母的品貌，
父母的神采……

样样看清楚，
永远记心怀。
再过多少年，
心里也自在。

明天这时候，
母亲黄土盖；
明天这时候，
爹爹坑里埋。

再过不多时，
一年和半载，
父母坟头上，
就要长青苔。

到了那时候，
烟消云散开。
要想见父母，
只好入梦来。

The corners of their mouths,
The shape of their faces;

Their clothes,
Their waist belts,
Their appearances and characters,
And their mien...

See everything clearly
And keep them in your heart forever.
Then no matter how many years will pass,
You will feel at ease.

At this time tomorrow,
Your mother will be covered with loess;
At this time tomorrow,
Your father will be buried.

Before long,
About a year or half,
On the grave mounds of your parents,
Mosses will grow.

By that time,
The fog and clouds will disperse.
If you want to see your parents,
You will have to do so in your dreams.

今天晚上呀，
你们快起来！
你们不起来，
莫把长老怪。

长老心最直，
长老口又快。
长老的话语，
包含多少爱！

你们今晚上，
诚心跪灵台。
孝服身上穿，
孝帕头上戴。

我要劝你们，
不要太伤怀，
不要哭倒地，
还要站起来！

长女和幼女，
父母最疼爱；
长子和幼子，
父母最疼爱。

你们今晚上，
都要站起来！

Tonight,

You hurry and get up!

If you do not,

Do not say the elders did not remind you.

The elders are the most forthright,

And the most outspoken.

The words of the elders,

Are filled with love for you!

You all tonight,

kneel in front of the altar sincerely.

Wear your mourning clothes

And your mourning hats.

I also urge you,

Not to be too sad,

Not to faint, to fall to the ground,

But to get back up!

The eldest and the youngest daughters

The parents loved most;

The eldest and the youngest sons

The parents loved most.

Tonight,

You all stand up!

看看父母亲，
父母也畅快。

父母也畅快，
你们也自在。
彼此无挂牵，
相安千万代。

黄叶落尽了，
新叶长起来。
父母去世了，
留得儿女在。

最好烧的柴，
算是麻栗柴。
只要点着火，
遍山烧起来。

我要祝你们，
日子像烧柴。
越烧火越旺，
火焰接云彩。

最易长的树，
不过是松柏。
种子落了地，
遍地长起来。

See your parents
And make them at ease.

If your parents are ease,
You will be at ease.
Without worrying about each other,
The family will be safe forever.

The dying leaves have all fallen,
And new leaves have grown out.
The parents have passed away,
And their children have carried on.

The easiest firewood to light
Is Mali①.
Once lit,
The whole mountain will be on fire.

My good wish to you is that
Your lives will be like the burning firewood.
The more it burns, the stronger it becomes,
Its flames touching the colorful clouds.

The easiest trees to grow
Are pines and cypresses.
Once the seeds fall to the ground,
The trees grow everywhere.

---

① A kind of tree.

我要祝你们，
子孙像松柏。
长得齐刷刷，
棵棵都成材。

最好种的菜，
不过是荞菜。
就是干坡地，
也会长起来。

我要祝你们，
六畜像荞菜，
满圈密匝匝，
年年都下崽。

孝子呀孝子，
对我莫见外。
我要对你们，
把心掏出来。

我既是长老，
就管村和寨。
你们相信我，
就得快起来！

My good wish to you is that

Your heirs will be like pines and cypresses.

They grow in unison,

Each one will be useful.

The easiest vegetable to grow

Is Qiaocai.

Even on dry slopes,

It still can thrive.

My good wish to you is that

Your six kinds of livestock will be like Qiaocai,

Filling up the pens,

Producing offspring every year.

Filial children,

Treat me not as an outsider.

To you I would like to,

Speak my mind.

Since I was an elder,

I manage the village affairs.

If you trust me,

Hurry and get up!